"Don't start that nonsense again, girl." Her grandmother slapped the arm of her chair.

"You will smile prettily and say yes when he asks for your hand in marriage. If you don't, you will invite my extreme displeasure."

"Come, now." Aunt Patricia's tones were as phlegmatic as ever. "It's not as if you can put Beatrice and Alexandra out of your home."

Alexandra cast a thankful glance in her aunt's direction. "I promise to work very hard, Grand-mère. I don't like being a burden to you, but I don't want to link my future with a man I do not love."

"Love!" Her grandmother spat the word. "Love is for commoners. You have a duty to your family. To all the children you will one day have. A duty you—will—not—forsake." The last three words were said with such emphasis that Alexandra winced.

DIANE ASHLEY, a "town girl" born and raised in Mississippi, has worked more than twenty years for the House of Representatives. She rediscovered a thirst for writing, was led to a class taught by Aaron McCarver, and became a founding member of the Bards of Faith. Visit her at www.bardsoffaith.homestead.com.

AARON McCARVER is a transplanted Mississippian who was raised in the mountains near Dunlap, Tennessee. He loves his jobs of teaching at two Christian colleges and editing for Barbour Publishing. A member of ACFW, he is coauthor with Gilbert Morris of the bestselling series, The Spirit of Appalachia.

Books by Diane Ashley and Aaron McCarver

HEARTSONG PRESENTS
HP860—Under the Tulip Poplar
HP879—A Bouquet for Iris
HP892—The Mockingbird's Call

Don't miss out on any of our super romances. Write to us at the following address for information on our newest releases and club information.

Heartsong Presents Readers' Service
PO Box 721
Uhrichsville, OH 44683

Or visit www.heartsongpresents.com

Across the Cotton Fields

Diane Ashley and Aaron McCarver

Heartsong Presents

To my Wesley College Family—From my years as a student through twenty years of ministry, God has used you all to enrich my life beyond measure. As our chorus says, "Wesley College, thou art owned of God. . . ." She is still a blessing to us all.

Aaron

For Mr. CJ and Mrs. Dorothy—Thanks for trusting me to care for your oldest son and welcoming me into your family with such warmth and love. You are the best parents-in-law in the world.

Diane

A note from the Authors:
We love to hear from our readers! You may correspond with us by writing:

Diane Ashley and Aaron McCarver
Author Relations
PO Box 721
Uhrichsville, OH 44683

ISBN 978-1-60260-955-6

ACROSS THE COTTON FIELDS

All scripture quotations are taken from the King James Version of the Bible.

All of the characters and events in this book are fictitious. Any resemblance to actual persons, living or dead, or to actual events is purely coincidental.

Our mission is to publish and distribute inspirational products offering exceptional value and biblical encouragement to the masses.

PRINTED IN THE U.S.A.

one

Nashville, Tennessee
August 1815

Alexandra Lewis sniffed and pressed a handkerchief against her dry lips. Would the tears ever stop? Or the pain? She wanted more than anything to go back to the time before. Before the world had changed. Before the sheriff had come to tell them about Papa's death. Before finding out the father she loved had been a liar, a thief. . .and a murderer.

How she wished she could just go to sleep and wake up to find the past week had been a terrible nightmare. But the sunlight pressing against her forehead and cheeks seemed real enough. Even though she didn't want to, Alexandra realized she would have to face the truth—their future was not going to be as easy as she had always imagined.

Tucking her handkerchief into the sleeve of her dress, Alexandra shifted her parasol to protect her face from the rays of the sun, then put her free arm around her mother. "It's okay, Mama. Everything is going to be okay."

Choked sobs answered her, but Mama leaned her head on Alexandra's shoulder. She sighed and patted her mother's back. Perhaps everything would be easier once they made it through the funeral service.

Not wanting to look toward the pine box that held her father's remains, Alexandra let her gaze roam across the grassy knoll on which she and her mother stood. No one else had come to support them in their grief, no one except the minister and his wife.

Alexandra lifted her chin and told herself they should be glad the whole town of Nashville was not here. As the townspeople had learned of the tragedy, they had taken pains to separate themselves from the Lewis ladies. Invitations no longer arrived, visitors no longer stopped by, and few notes of condolence found their way to the house.

It was not surprising given her father's actions, but Alexandra wished at least one or two of the people she considered particular friends had decided to come. Like Asher Landon, for example. He had been a frequent visitor in the weeks before. . .before the nightmare. But from what Mama was told, he was there the day Papa's villainy had been exposed. Perhaps he didn't want to be near her anymore.

If only Papa had not been so greedy, so anxious to enter the world of politics. His desire to be elected to a political position had led him to have a family of settlers murdered so he could obtain their land and fulfill the qualifications needed to run for office. He then covered up his atrocities by making it appear the settlers had been attacked by an Indian living outside of Nashville. When his murderous actions were uncovered, he was killed in a shootout with Asher and Sheriff McGhee.

Did Asher think so little of her that he had no condolences to offer her and her mother? Or had he been influenced by Rebekah, the unsophisticated girl who wanted to drag him to the country? Alexandra lifted her chin. No matter. She didn't need the Landons or any of the other townspeople to survive.

The sound of a carriage coming toward them distracted her from her thoughts. Curiosity made her turn her head. Three people disembarked. She recognized the young woman as someone she'd met at parties. Dorothea? No, Dorcas. That was it—Dorcas Montgomery. A beanpole of a girl with blond hair and a pale complexion. Although they had met, she didn't really consider Dorcas a friend.

The girl nodded to her, and Alexandra tried to summon a smile. Perhaps she did have friends here in Nashville. Perhaps not everyone in town thought she and her mother were as guilty as Papa. Maybe the Montgomerys understood why his family mourned a man who had committed such awful deeds.

Of course no one knew Papa like she did. But even she couldn't understand why he had gotten involved. Had someone else forced him to take those dreadful actions? Or had he simply become a madman?

How could she reconcile his actions with the loving father she had grown up adoring? What had happened to the man who'd ordered a fancy officer's uniform and joined the ragged troops who defended New Orleans from British invasion? The man who had comforted and protected her his whole life? When had he lost his way? And why hadn't she seen the truth when she could have helped him, perhaps even prevented his death?

"At a time such as this, many verses can bring comfort to a grieving heart." The minister, Roman Miller, opened his Bible and began to read from the book of Psalms. "'God is our refuge and strength, a very present help in trouble. Therefore will not we fear, though the earth be removed, and though the mountains be carried into the midst of the sea; though the waters thereof roar and be troubled, though the mountains shake with the swelling thereof. Selah.'"

He flipped through some pages and began reading again. "'Fear thou not; for I am with thee: be not dismayed; for I am thy God: I will strengthen thee; yea, I will help thee; yea, I will uphold thee with the right hand of my righteousness.'"

The words flowed around her, and something in Alexandra's chest eased a tiny bit. Perhaps she and Mama would recover from the disgrace, the shame, and the grief.

A voice, cold and heartless, seemed to whisper in her ear. People said God would provide for them. They said He was all powerful, all knowing. So why would He have let her father do something so horrible? Why hadn't He stopped all this from happening? Why was He punishing them?

The peaceful feeling slipped away, replaced by bitterness. The last few days had shown Alexandra the only one she could rely on was herself. She bowed her head when the minister said they should, but she blocked out his words. She didn't want to be lied to. . .not anymore. From now on, she only wanted to hear the whole, unvarnished truth.

"Alexandra?" Her mother's voice seemed to come from far away.

She looked up to see the others staring at her. "I'm sorry." She could feel a flush burning her cheeks. "It's. . .I. . ."

"Everything will be all right." Mrs. Miller smiled gently. "Getting lost in prayer is not a bad thing."

Mr. and Mrs. Montgomery offered their condolences to Mama, while Dorcas stepped over to her. Her hazel gaze speared Alexandra. "I'm so sorry for your loss."

Alexandra felt exposed, as if Dorcas was searching for some sign to report to her friends back in town. She could almost hear the whispered discussion—the exclamations of shock, the *tsk*s and titters of revulsion as Dorcas and the others in town analyzed every word she spoke, every action she made. She dug her fingernails into her clenched hands and managed a nod. "Thank you."

Mama reached for her arm. "We should get back home. People may have come by the house, and they'll wonder where we are."

Alexandra's heart dropped to her toes. Was her mother also losing her mind? Or was it grief that made her forget the lack of visitors? Should she agree? Or correct her mother?

While she was still trying to decide what to do, Pastor Miller held both arms out, one for his wife, one for Mama.

Alexandra followed them to the carriage, her eyes on the headstones of other men and women who had been buried in the cemetery. The beautiful setting was lost on her, even though she could hear the gurgle of a nearby stream. Instead of bringing comfort, its murmur seemed to reinforce her fear and loss. What would they do now that they had no man to lead the household?

⁂

The busy waterfront streets of New Orleans gave way to tall trees and marsh grasses as Jeremiah LeGrand neared

L'Hôpital des Pauvres de la Charité, the newly reconstructed charity hospital that first opened in 1736. Charity Hospital had originally been located in town at the intersection of Chartres and Bienville streets, but this was its fourth location since it outgrew its original building. The three-story structure was sturdy, with a line of wide, arched doorways at the ground level, but complaints had already been made about inadequate care and meager supplies because of the hospital's remote location. Jeremiah had his doubts about the decision to rebuild the hospital in the middle of the swamps, but he supposed the leaders knew what they were doing.

He stepped through wide double doors that stood open in hopes of capturing a cool breeze. It was only a few degrees cooler inside, but at least the sun no longer pounded on his shoulders. He nodded to a white-robed nun on his way to the ward on the second floor, glad he no longer had to explain his presence. Because of his frequent visits, the staff allowed him access without question.

He hoped to find his friend up and about this afternoon, practicing walking with his crutches, but Judah was still abed. Apparently the ceiling was filled with interesting designs. It certainly held his friend's total attention. Judah's arms were crossed beneath his head, and Jeremiah saw his light brown hair had been pulled back into an old-fashioned queue and tied with a strip of leather. His ruddy complexion had faded over the past months due to his inability to leave the hospital, but Jeremiah hoped that would change before long. The doctor had told them last week that the contagion was cured—Judah's leg had healed. All he needed now was a way home.

Removing his hat, Jeremiah tucked it under one arm. "Good afternoon." Sympathy washed through him as he watched his friend jerk a sheet over his legs. He tried to put himself in Judah's place, tried to imagine not having two strong legs to hold himself up. His stomach clenched, and he sent a silent thanks to God for blessing him with excellent health.

"Hi." Judah's greeting had a surly ring.

"I've brought you a surprise."

Judah's expression changed from a dissatisfied frown to a tentative smile. "Is it a letter from home?"

Jeremiah nodded, and his smile broadened. He held out several folded pieces of vellum that had been sealed with a blob of red wax.

The other man took them from him, but he didn't break the seal as Jeremiah had expected.

"Aren't you going to read it?"

"Later. I want to savor every word."

Jeremiah spied a wooden chair under one window and dragged it over to the cot. "How are you feeling?"

A sigh raised Judah's shoulders. "Sometimes it feels as if my leg is still there. But when I reach down. . .there's nothing."

"I'm so sorry. Is there anything I can do?"

"Give me back my leg."

Now it was Jeremiah's turn to sigh. "We've been through this so many times, Judah."

Judah turned his face away. "I know I should be happy to be alive, but how can I be? Here I am stuck in this steamy swamp for more than half a year while my wife is struggling to keep body and soul together at Magnolia Plantation. If I was any kind of real man, I'd have gotten back to Natchez long before now."

"I'm certain the note from your wife will hold no hint of censure."

"Of course not. My Susannah is an absolute angel. But she cannot run our plantation without my help."

"You've told me how good your overseer is. He will have helped her in your absence." Jeremiah shifted on the hard chair. "Judah, you must get past blaming yourself. It's not your fault that you were wounded. Nor is it your fault your leg didn't heal properly. I know it's been hard, but you should be able to go home soon."

A bitter laugh greeted his statement. "I can't even walk

across the room. How can you expect me to get all the way to Natchez? I cannot ride a horse with only one good leg. Do you think I can paddle my way against the river currents?" He shook his head. "I need a job so I can earn the money for a carriage. I probably won't be able to make the trip home until after the end of the year. Susannah needs me now, not five months from now."

"You know I can help. I'll gladly loan you a carriage or the money to lease one. You can repay me whenever you get back on your feet."

Judah slapped his leg, the one that had been amputated below the knee. "That's just it. I'll never get back on my feet. I only have one."

Jeremiah winced at the anger in his friend's voice. "I cannot imagine how hard the past months have been for you, but if you will only turn your mind to the fact you still have so much. Look around you at the other men in this hospital. Most of them have no home to go to. Most of them would trade places with you in an instant."

Silence answered him. It drew longer and tighter as the seconds ticked by. Finally Judah nodded. "You're right, of course. I sometimes forget."

"I cannot blame you for that. You've had many trials."

"And a wonderful friend to keep me from becoming too morose."

Jeremiah ducked his head for a moment before meeting his friend's gaze. "If the situation was reversed, you would do the same for me." He hesitated for a moment before going on. "I promise you this, Judah. I won't insult you by offering you money, but I have an idea or two about how to help you get home before the harvest is over."

"An idea, huh?" Judah reached for the crutches leaning against the wall next to his bed. "If I'm to get home anytime soon, I'm going to have to become proficient on these things."

They spent the next two hours traversing the distance from one end of the hospital to the other. They stopped to talk to the other patients, dispensing hope and laughter as they went. By the time Jeremiah took his leave, he and his friend were laughing with the abandonment of young boys.

He still had no idea how to keep his promise to Judah, but he prayed God would show him a way.

two

Visiting the hospital every day got more difficult as Mississippi River traffic increased. It seemed the growing number of boats appearing at the dock fueled the demand for goods instead of quenching it. And the few steamboats that traveled down and up the river so speedily could not handle all the demand. Every boat was filled, from the most rustic canoe to oceangoing schooners and brigantines. Trading was brisk and lucrative for everyone involved, but work filled almost every waking hour for Jeremiah and his uncle.

The shadows lengthened in the narrow streets, signaling the end to another day. Jeremiah locked the front door and leaned against it wearily.

"Eh, *neveu*, you are too young to be so tired." Uncle Emile stepped away from his desk. He was a short man, with a much darker head of hair and complexion than his nephew. He reminded Jeremiah very much of his father, who had died years ago during an outbreak of typhus. The same outbreak that took Jeremiah's mother. It had swept through New Orleans more than a decade ago, sparing neither the rich nor the poor. Then the following year, *Tante* Jeanne had died in childbirth along with the baby boy who would have been Uncle Emile's heir. Now there were only the two of them. The devastating losses they had faced had made them closer than many fathers and sons.

"It's been a busy week," Jeremiah stated the obvious. "Why don't you go upstairs and see what Marguerite has prepared for our dinner? The smells from up there have been making my mouth water for the past hour. I will put away the ledger and make sure we are ready for an early start tomorrow."

When Jeremiah finally climbed the stairs, his stomach was

growling loudly enough to make someone think a bear was outside. He took his usual place at the dining table, at Uncle Emile's right hand.

Marguerite, the diminutive woman who cooked and cleaned for them, fussed with the soup tureen, ladling a fragrant stew onto his plate. "It's about time you got here, *petit*." She put a hand on her hip and frowned. "I was beginning to think you did not like *la cuisine* I have prepared."

Jeremiah let his mouth drop in surprise. "Have I ever not liked what you cook, tante?" He used the term of endearment even though Marguerite was not his aunt. From time to time he had even thought Uncle Emile might propose to her, but he never did. Would his uncle ever recover from the loss of his wife and child? It was a request he often took to the Lord, but so far, no result had been forthcoming.

Marguerite slapped him on the back with her serving cloth. "This is very true. You have a good appetite, not like your *oncle* who only picks at his food."

Uncle Emile huffed and patted his flat stomach. "I eat more than enough. I think you just want to fatten me up like a cow to be slaughtered."

All three of them laughed. It was a discussion often repeated at the dinner table. Marguerite shook her head and left them to their dinner. Uncle Emile blessed the food and tucked his napkin into the collar of his shirt.

Jeremiah tasted the savory stew, relishing the spicy blend of seafood and fresh vegetables. "Delicious."

"Yes, Marguerite has outdone herself." Uncle Emile picked up a plate of corn bread and passed it to Jeremiah.

The clock on the wall, an import from Germany, ticked loudly as the two men ate in companionable silence. Marguerite came back to remove the stew and serve a rich torte for dessert. Then she offered coffee, a rich, dark blend that complimented the sweet cake.

When they had both satisfied their hunger, Jeremiah and Uncle Emile retired to the parlor.

"You seem preoccupied tonight, Jeremiah. Is there something on your mind?"

Wondering how to express the general feeling of dissatisfaction that had been dogging him for the past week, Jeremiah sighed.

"I know." Uncle Emile clapped his knee and laughed. "Only a woman can bring such a sigh, neveu. Who is she? Why have I not heard of her?"

"Oh no, Uncle, it's not that at all." Jeremiah could feel his cheeks flush. "I just feel. . .I don't know. . .pointless, I guess."

His uncle steepled his hands under his chin. "Ah, I see." A frown drew his eyebrows together. "No, I do not see. You have a challenging job, an important one in my business, and more money than you care to spend. What is there to make you feel so aimless?"

Jeremiah nodded. "You're right, of course. I have many reasons to be thankful. God is faithful. He has filled my life with blessings."

"By the time I was your age, I already knew that I wanted to be a business magnate. Even as a young boy in Quebec City, I dreamed of marrying a special girl, bringing her to New Orleans, and running a successful enterprise."

"And you've accomplished all of that."

Uncle Emile closed his eyes for a moment before answering. "My only disappointment is that my beloved Jeanne did not live long enough to enjoy all this." He opened his eyes then and smiled at Jeremiah. "But *le bon Dieu* still arranged to give me a beloved son."

"Thank you, Uncle Emile." Jeremiah reached out a hand and gripped his relative's blunt fingers. "You've been wonderful to me."

"But. . ." Uncle Emile sighed and pulled his hand away. "It is not enough."

The words fell between them like boulders.

Jeremiah's stomach clenched. He didn't want to hurt his uncle, but the pull to do something more with his life was strong. He had prayed many times about the desire to break away from his uncle's business. New Orleans was an exciting place to live, filled with people from all walks of life, from different countries and different backgrounds. Many opportunities existed to help others here, but no matter what Jeremiah involved himself in, it was not enough. He wanted to do more. "I've been praying about this and looking for what God wants me to do, and I think I have an idea."

Uncle Emile sat back in his chair. "I don't know if I want to find out about this grand idea of yours, but I suppose I have no choice."

"That's not true." Jeremiah pushed back from the table. He had no wish to bring pain to the man who had raised him. He would continue looking until he found a way to follow God's calling without hurting his uncle. "I can keep my own counsel."

"Sit down." The older man did not raise his voice, but the command was obvious from his brisk tone. "I want to hear your ideas."

Jeremiah complied. He took a moment to pray for the right words to explain his dream to his relative. It was crucial to him to have Uncle Emile's blessing.

"You know how hard it was when *Maman* and Papa died. I. . .I was so lost." He swallowed hard. This explanation was more difficult than he had imagined it would be, but perhaps the only way to convince his uncle was to show his vulnerability. "Until you brought me to your home, I thought I would have to live on the streets."

"I would never have let that happen."

"I know that, Uncle Emile, and I will always be grateful. Please believe that. But not every child has a loving uncle to raise him. Some of those children do end up on the streets. Some of them starve, while others die of disease. Most often, the ones who do not perish become criminals. They are forced into hopelessness through no fault of their own. They become pickpockets and thieves—angry and lost because no one has offered them shelter or love."

He glanced up to see his uncle's reaction. The older man's face seemed to have become a mask. It was wiped clean of any emotion. What was he thinking? Was he offended by Jeremiah's desire to walk away from the family business? Would he support his nephew's desire? Or quash it?

Silence filled the room once again, like a third presence.

Jeremiah wished he had not been so honest, but the desire to explain his dream had been growing for months now.

"You wish to work with the Ursuline nuns at the orphan asylum?" The frown had returned to his uncle's face.

"No. I have no wish to interfere with the work of the Catholic Church, but the need is greater than even the nuns can meet." Jeremiah swallowed hard. "I want to establish a place—a home. I would like for it to be a large house in the country. That way, I could offer a safe haven to dozens of orphans. My dream is to offer them a refuge where the children can run and play and learn about the love of their heavenly Father."

"I see. So you are planning to leave New Orleans?"

"I don't know. I haven't gotten that far with my plans. But most of the land here is either fields for planters or swamps."

"You told me you have promised to help your friend return to Natchez, *n'est-ce pas?*"

Now it was Jeremiah's turn to frown. What did helping Judah have to do with any of this? "That trip will be only a matter of a few days if we can procure seats on one of the steamships going north."

Uncle Emile pushed his chair back from the table. He walked toward the fireplace, unlit at this time of year, and stood with his back to Jeremiah.

The silence returned.

Jeremiah picked up the linen napkin he had laid next to his plate earlier and twisted it in his hands. He wanted to say more, but something stopped him.

After a few moments, his uncle turned back to him. "I have an idea."

Jeremiah looked up at the man who had been a father to him for the majority of his life. Were the lines on his forehead deeper than they had been earlier? Was he hurting because Jeremiah had shared his dream, or was he just in deep thought?

"I have been thinking for some time of opening a new office up the river, but I do not have the time to explore for the best location and trustworthy employees. Perhaps you should plan to make your trip to Natchez more extended. Although the port may be similar to the area around New Orleans, who knows? If the area seems to have promise, perhaps you can build this house you dream of at the same time you establish a new office for our business. If trade continues to increase as I foresee, you should have more than enough money to build this orphanage and hire half the town of Natchez to watch over the children."

Jeremiah's heart soared. Why hadn't he thought of this solution already? "Uncle Emile, you are brilliant." Jeremiah stood and walked over to where his uncle stood, placing an arm around the shorter man's shoulders. "I can take Judah home, find land to build on, and not feel like I am deserting you. This is perfect. I can see the house now, big and comfortable and overlooking the river. You will have to come and stay with me as soon as it is built." Jeremiah grinned at his uncle. "I wish I had told you sooner."

"Let this be a lesson to you, neveu."

Jeremiah knew his uncle well enough to know he was having a hard time keeping a smile from his face.

His uncle shook a finger at him. "Just because I am old does not mean I am senile. I still have a few good ideas left."

"You are the smartest man I know."

Emile inclined his head toward the door. "Go on, now. You have many plans to make if you are to accomplish your dreams."

three

Jemma opened the door a few inches and slipped into the parlor. "Mr. McKinley has arrived, madam."

Alexandra's mother waved a handkerchief toward her daughter. In the six weeks since Papa's funeral, Mama had retreated further and further into a world of silence.

Alexandra sighed and wondered how she had become the one to make all the decisions. "Show him in, Jemma."

"Yes, miss."

As Jemma left the room, Alexandra couldn't help but wonder if this slave who had been a part of their household for as long as she could remember would still be with them given a chance to leave. Everyone else had deserted them.

Jemma quickly returned with the attorney, who had sent them a note requesting a meeting. He was about Papa's age, but the similarity stopped there. Where Papa had been somewhat rotund with a clean-shaven face, Mr. McKinley was tall and fit. He sported a neat mustache that matched his brown hair. He seemed to fill the room with his presence. From the shine on his square-toed shoes to his well-pressed suit, everything about the man screamed money. He walked to the table that took up one corner of the parlor and placed a large portfolio on it before turning and bowing to both of them. "I am sorry for your loss, Mrs. Lewis, Miss Lewis."

Mama pressed her handkerchief to her face, leaving Alexandra to acknowledge the man.

"Thank you, Mr. McKinley." The phrase was not as hard to voice now that a little time had passed. "It's a pleasure to meet you. Papa spoke highly of you."

"Thank you."

"We were a bit surprised at your note requesting a meeting."

Alexandra softened her voice to make sure he would not take her comment as displeasure. "We would always be delighted to welcome you into our home."

"Yes." Mama's face reappeared for a moment. "Have you come to tell us the latest news of town? We do not hear any gossip these days."

The attorney looked a bit surprised at her mother's question, but he apparently found it impossible to disappoint her. "I did hear of a wedding last week of one of the town's most eligible bachelors. Nothing fancy, mind you. It was apparently a simple affair out in the country at the bride's home. Perhaps you know the couple—Asher Landon and Rebekah Taylor?"

Alexandra could feel the blood drain from her face. "Yes. . .I do know them." She pasted a smile on her face, but her heart, already torn from the scandal surrounding her father, shattered into a million tiny pieces. Everything fell into place. Asher had not attended the funeral or visited them because he'd been too busy courting his old sweetheart. He had toyed with her heart, led her on. Well, she hoped Rebekah would make him utterly miserable. A flash of guilt pierced her. Asher was an honorable man. She had been the one trying to draw his affections away from the woman he'd known all his life. But after all, Alexandra convinced herself, Asher would have been better off choosing her for a wife. She could have done more for his career in a month than that pale, simplistic woman could do in a year. "How nice for them."

"Yes, well. . ." Mr. McKinley cleared his throat. He must have realized his choice of topic was not a good one. "I am afraid the reason for my visit is not as pleasant." He stopped again. "I am sorry, but I have some rather bad news to share with you ladies."

Mama looked up, her hazel eyes damp. "Whatever do you mean, sir?"

"The news I have for you ladies is not going to help you recover from your grief."

Alexandra's heart started to pound. She didn't know how

much more she could take. "Perhaps you should sit down, sir, and tell us this news. No matter how hard it is, we must know the truth."

Mr. McKinley nodded and took a seat in one of the chairs facing the settee. "I have paid all the bills your creditors have presented to me over the past three months, but I regret to tell you that I will not be able to do so any longer."

"Why is that, sir?" Alexandra was somewhat surprised by her aggressiveness. A year ago she never would have dreamed of questioning the family solicitor. But now she had little choice. "Are you retiring?"

He rubbed his mustache with one finger. "No, of course not."

"Have we done something to offend you?"

"No. I was shocked at the news of your father's doings, but I have never thought the worse of you ladies."

"Exactly what is the problem then?"

"To put it bluntly, miss, there is no money."

Her mother gasped and sank back, covering her whole face with her handkerchief and moaning.

"Mama, I think you should consider retiring. I can meet with Mr. McKinley and talk about our situation. I'm certain we can work something out." Alexandra stood up and walked across the room to pull the rope that would summon Jemma.

When the slave arrived, Alexandra directed her to escort her mother upstairs and return with refreshments as soon as possible. The woman nodded and coaxed her mother up from the settee, cooing and murmuring to her as she helped her from the room.

After they departed, Alexandra took a deep breath. "I apologize, Mr. McKinley. Mama is not herself these days. Now, where were we?"

"I was telling you that the small amount of money your father deposited with me before. . .before he died. . .has been exhausted. Unless a large sum is available that I am not aware of, the two of you are near poverty."

Alexandra closed her eyes. When would the difficulties

stop? She wanted to scream her frustration. She was barely a grown woman. Why must all this fall in her lap? What had happened to the easy life she had once enjoyed? Was it gone forever? Would things improve?

She looked at the stylish furniture she and her mother had selected for their home. She didn't want to give up everything. It was too hard to think of losing all of the things that made them comfortable.

Perhaps there was another way. It wouldn't be easy, but it might be less painful than giving up everything. "Could we sell this house? Perhaps we can buy or even lease a smaller one. If we are careful with our expenses, we should be able to get by."

Mr. McKinley shook his head, his eyes sorrowful. "Your father mortgaged the house."

"What?"

"Your father borrowed against the value of the house. I have to assume he was trying to amass money for some special purpose. But whatever his goal, I am afraid it will remain out of reach for his loved ones. You simply do not have sufficient money for the two of you to survive by yourselves."

Alexandra pushed herself up from the settee and wandered around the room, her mind spinning.

"Not everyone trusts banks to hold their money. Perhaps your father secreted a large amount of cash about the house? Perhaps in a safe?"

She considered the suggestion, hoping it might be valid, but shook her head after a few moments. "We've gone through P—my father's study, sorting through his papers. We have not found a safe or any appreciable amount of cash."

"I see." The lawyer walked over to the table and pulled papers out of the portfolio he had brought. He drew a pair of spectacles from the inside pocket of his coat and settled them on his nose. "Then I am afraid your situation is rather bleak."

He showed Alexandra lists of expenses and assets until her head was nearly spinning. She rubbed her temples to ease a throbbing pain there. "So if we sell everything, how much will we have?"

Mr. McKinley took in a deep breath. "Not much, I'm afraid. Do you have any family who can help you through this. . .difficult time?"

Alexandra looked out the window. "We do not have family in Tennessee." She watched the lazy downward journey of an oak leaf as an errant wind blew it loose from its limb. How nice it would be to have someone here to rely on. "Papa brought us here because General Jackson wanted him here. I once hoped I might marry into one of the local families, but after the trouble. . ." She let the words drift off. This man surely understood her meaning. Her social hopes had been dashed as soon as word had leaked out about her father's "indiscretion."

Alexandra knew what Papa had done was more than an indiscretion, but it was the only term she allowed herself to use when thinking of his actions. She wished more than anything that she could start afresh, but—

An idea came to her then. Why had she not thought of it sooner? She turned to look into the attorney's grave countenance. "Do you think we could amass enough money to pay for passage on one of the steamships?"

"Passage to what destination?"

"We have family in Natchez." Alexandra could feel her heart thumping. It was the answer to everything. She and Mama could move in with *Grand-mère*. No one down in the Mississippi territory would have heard about Papa's indiscretion. They would be able to start anew.

"I'm certain that can be arranged." The attorney smiled at her, relief apparent on his features.

"Everything really is going to be all right." She pushed back from the pile of confusing papers and stood up. Her mind began to imagine going to Tanner Plantation.

The attorney barely had time to get all his things together before she practically shoved him out the front door. He told her he thought he knew of a buyer for the house. That would relieve the greatest financial burden. And since they were going to leave anyway, it hardly mattered.

As soon as the man was gone, she skipped upstairs to tell her mother what they were going to do. The townspeople of Nashville were no longer of any concern. Even Asher. Let him have his Rebekah. Perhaps one of these days, she would return to Nashville on the arm of her wealthy, influential husband. Then they would see who had made the best of their circumstances.

four

Fog wafted pale and cool over the brown river as the steamship churned its way into the port at Natchez. Alexandra clutched the edges of her cape and imagined that the mournful steamship whistle must sound like the cry of lost souls. She shivered, her gaze combing the bank ahead for a sign of one of her relatives.

Plenty of people scurried about even though the hour was advanced. The sun had not yet set, but she wasn't sure it would still be light by the time the steamship made landfall. Steamers might be the fastest vessels on the river, but this captain was very wary of snags and took a long time bringing his boat to shore. She supposed she ought to be grateful for his caution. They had experienced a very uneventful trip from Nashville to the Mississippi Territory.

The fog dampened her hair and clothing before sliding silently onto the bank. It obscured her view and gave an otherworldly feel to the late afternoon. Of course, it also softened the outlines of the ragged buildings, turning the shacks into hazy outlines that might have been fancy homes.

Alexandra could not see any sign of her relatives. She turned and headed back to the cabin she and her mother had shared for the past weeks. Jemma, the only slave who remained after they sold off their property, was folding their clothes and putting them away in one of the many trunks they had brought along. It was a good thing they had ordered new wardrobes before they found out about their financial situation or she and Mama would have been clothed in inappropriately bright colors.

Mama sat in one corner of the room, a kerosene lantern casting its yellow glow on her shoulders and the needlework in her lap. "Hi, dear."

"It's foggy and cool outside." Alexandra pulled her cloak off and dropped it on the bed that took up most of the room. "But we're almost there. Soon we'll be resting at Grand-mère's home."

"Yes." Mama's smile was shaky and seemed to be growing weaker with each day that passed, each mile that drew them closer to Natchez.

The mournful tones of the steamboat's whistle made all three women jump. Jemma closed the first chest and moved to another one. "Can't get off this boat soon enough fer me."

Alexandra put a hand out to keep herself upright as the steamboat lurched slightly. "Me either." She turned to look at her mother. "I didn't see anyone I know waiting for us, Mama. Do you think we'll have help when we disembark?"

Mama's smile disappeared. She wrung her hands. "Oh my. What will we do if they're not here? I don't know how we'll manage. Everything was so much easier when your father was alive."

"It will be all right, Mama." Alexandra shrugged. "I will find a carriage or a wagon. There must be someone who will be willing to take us to the plantation."

Mama grabbed her handkerchief, never far away, and started to cry.

Alexandra wanted to lash out at her, but she was so pitiful. Life would be much easier if Mama would take a little responsibility, but it seemed that was beyond her. Alexandra had arranged their passage with the help of the nice lawyer. She and Jemma had gone on board early to make certain the accommodations were acceptable. Then they had returned to the house and packed up the clothes and other meager belongings that had not been sold. All the while, Mama sat and stared out the window or wept into her handkerchief.

"Jemma, I have spoken to the captain about getting our things on shore. He assured me there would be no problem. We'll all go ashore, and I'll leave you to watch over Mama while I find a carriage or wagon, some kind of conveyance to get us home."

Jemma's eyes widened, but she nodded.

Alexandra sent her an encouraging smile. She had been a jewel during the trip. In fact, Alexandra didn't know if she could have made it without her help.

Alexandra grabbed Mama's cloak and coaxed her to stand and let it be draped around her shoulders. When she was certain Mama was suitably wrapped up, she pulled her own cloak on and helped her mother negotiate the steps leading to the deck. It only took a few more moments before the boat was secured and the loading plank was swung over to the bank.

"Let's go, Mama." Alexandra took a tentative step and flung her arms out for balance. "See how easy this is." She beckoned for Mama and Jemma to follow. All three of them made it safely to shore and looked around.

Natchez Under-the-Hill. Alexandra had heard stories of the area. It was a hiding place for gamblers, criminals, and lawless men, most of them running from New Orleans justice. It was no place for two ladies to spend any amount of time. Well, she'd better remedy that situation before it got any darker.

After repeating her instructions to Jemma and her mother, Alexandra walked toward the nearest building, hoping she would find it to be a livery stable. A woman who looked even more bedraggled than Alexandra felt stepped outside. When questioned, she pointed the way toward a stable a few blocks toward the east, away from the river.

The fog swirled around her legs as she walked, obscuring the ground and making it difficult for her to see where she was going. Hoping the woman had directed her correctly, Alexandra turned a corner and found herself in a quieter part of town. Buildings rose up on either side of her, their shadows lengthening as full dark began to settle on them.

A horseshoe hanging from a metal rod indicated that

a building ahead was the one she sought. Intent on her destination, Alexandra hurried forward, hope singing through her. But disaster struck when she put her foot into an unseen rut and twisted her ankle. A shriek of pain and fear broke through her lips as she fell, landing with a jarring *thump*.

It took her a minute to recover her senses, and when she did, she groaned. She was covered in mud and dirt, her hat drooped to one side, and her cloak was torn in several places. She dragged herself up with some effort and leaned against the nearest wall, ignoring the bite of splinters that pierced her gloved hands. Her breath came in labored spurts, and the street seemed to move as though it had turned into the river.

Several minutes passed, but finally the street regained its solidity and her breathing settled into a more normal pace. She pushed away from the wall and put her full weight on her injured foot. Pain shot up her leg, causing her to fall back once more. At least this time the street did not waver, but she knew her situation was serious. Her mother was counting on her. She could not fail. She wanted to sink to the ground and sob, but crying would not help the situation. What was she going to do?

How many blocks had she walked in her search? She wasn't certain. She could no longer see the waterfront, or Mama and Jemma. And no one seemed to be around in this dark, narrow corridor. Alexandra closed her eyes. *God, help me.* The words formed in her mind even though she didn't really believe He would answer her plea.

A sound to her right made Alexandra's eyes fly open. Two men rounded the corner and lurched toward her. They appeared to be drunk, leaning on each other and weaving their way up the street. The drunker of the two was shorter, and he was moving in an odd hopping fashion while leaning against his taller companion.

"Come along, Judah," the taller one encouraged his companion. "We're almost at the stable where we're supposed to rendezvous with your lady."

Alexandra was surprised at the lack of slurring in the man's voice. At least he wasn't drunk. He must be helping his master home. She remembered seeing other boats at the landing. Perhaps this pair had arrived on one of them.

As they drew closer she realized the shorter man, a soldier by his garb, was moving oddly because he had lost the lower part of his right leg. She pressed a hand to her mouth, sympathy for his plight filling her. Suddenly her twisted ankle seemed a minor inconvenience.

The smaller man looked up and saw her. "What have we here? A lady in distress?"

The servant stared at her boldly, his gaze taking in her torn clothing and the spatters of mud on her face. "More likely a lady of the streets."

Alexandra's mouth fell open in shock. She closed it with a snap and directed her attention to the soldier. "You should teach your man to bridle his tongue. It will do neither of you any good to allow him to criticize his betters." She would have liked to turn her shoulder on both of them and stalk away, but the throbbing in her ankle halted her.

What the soldier's answer might have been was muffled by the sound of horses' hooves approaching. A carriage rounded the corner. Alexandra shrank back against her wall, biting her lip to keep from moaning as her leg throbbed once more.

The carriage came to an abrupt halt as it drew even with the two men, and a blond whirlwind emerged from it. The woman was even smaller than the soldier, but what she lacked in stature she made up for in energy. She ran to the soldier and threw her arms around him.

"Careful, or you'll overset him," the manservant warned.

"Praise God for bringing you home to me." The lady placed a kiss on the lame man's cheek before turning to his companion. "And Jeremiah, how can I ever thank you for your duty to my husband? He has written to me of your bravery and constancy. No amount of money could ever repay you for what you have done."

"It is my pleasure." The tall man smiled down at the blond woman, and Alexandra caught her breath. His features, which she had considered harsh, were transformed. His hair fell forward across his broad forehead, his lips curved upward and revealed a pair of dimples, and his warm gaze made her toes curl even though it was not directed at her.

"Oh, it is so good to see you both. Judah, my love, you cannot imagine how much I have missed you all these months. I cannot wait to get you home. You look so pale, dear. But we'll take care of that in a matter of days."

"Susannah, I have missed you so."

The words were filled with such emotion that Alexandra felt like an interloper. For a moment she wished someone missed her that much. Even though Asher Landon had been kind to her, he had never shown her the same depth of emotion. Suddenly she was truly glad he had decided to marry elsewhere. Perhaps one day she would meet a man who loved her as much as this man loved his wife. Alexandra shifted her weight to ease her discomfort, wishing once again for the ability to walk away.

The lady noticed her for the first time. "Who is this?"

The soldier shook his head. "I was about to find out if she needed our help when you arrived, dearest."

"I'm trying to find the livery stable. I need to hire someone to get me and my mother to Tanner Plantation."

"Tanner Plantation?" The blond lady peered up at her. "Are you a relative of the Tanners?"

Alexandra nodded. "My mother was a Tanner before she married. My. . .my father died recently and we—"

"Oh, you poor thing," the lady broke in on her explanation. She turned back to her husband. "We must help them, Judah."

Jeremiah shook his head. "You are too trusting. If she was who she claims, her family would be here to meet her and her mother. You should send her to the livery stable." He pointed to the horseshoe a few feet away.

The harsh words brought a rush of tears to Alexandra's

eyes. If only she could slap this impertinent servant. What had the world come to that such as he was allowed to speak so to a lady?

No matter how badly it hurt, she would not stay here one moment longer. Setting her jaw, she pushed away from the wall. If she was very careful, surely she could make it. She ignored the threesome and stepped forward on her good foot, but when she took her next step, the pain overwhelmed her. The light from the carriage faded, as did the voices of the strangers, and she pitched forward once more.

❧

A pungent smell made Alexandra's head jerk back against a solid shoulder. Mama had burned a feather and was waving it under her nose.

"There, she's coming to now." A puff of air tickled her ear. The voice was unfamiliar, but the cadence of his words was not. For a moment she believed she was back in New Orleans right after the war. Papa was still alive, and everything else was naught but a strange dream.

Reality pushed her hopes aside as Alexandra opened her eyes to find herself inside a strange carriage. She was not in New Orleans; she was in Natchez. . .Natchez Under-the-Hill. She struggled against the arms holding her but could not break free. Horror stories of unwary victims being snatched from the streets and robbed—or worse—came to life in her mind. Her movements grew more frantic, but the arms were more like iron bonds than flesh and blood.

"Jeremiah, let go." A woman's voice came from the opposite bench. "Can't you see you're frightening her?"

Instantly she was free. Alexandra dragged herself as far away from him as she could manage and stared at the people inside the carriage.

The crippled soldier and his wife sat opposite her, while the rude servant sat on her side, his arms now folded across his wide chest.

"Where am I?"

The soldier smiled at her. "You blacked out, my dear. Jeremiah here caught you and transported you to safety."

Her fears faded somewhat. The couple's concern seemed genuine.

His wife leaned forward and placed a hand on her arm. "We would like to see you and your mother safely to your destination."

"I still think you should hire a separate wagon for them if you are so determined to be taken in by this woman's tale."

She could hear the censure in the servant's—Jeremiah's—voice. But he had a valid point. "Perhaps he's right."

"Nonsense, just tell us where to find your mother." The woman smiled at her. "We will take care of the rest."

Alexandra could not resist her friendliness. And she was so tired. And her foot was throbbing. So she directed them to the waterfront.

It took a few moments to find her mother, who had become distraught at Alexandra's long absence. But after explaining the chain of events and providing introductions all around, it was settled. Alexandra and her mother would ride inside the carriage with their new friends, Judah and Susannah Hughes. Jemma and Jeremiah would ride up front next to the driver as soon as he and Jeremiah stowed all of the luggage.

Their arrival at Tanner Plantation caused a flurry of activity. Uncle John and Aunt Patricia welcomed them as Grand-mère had already retired. Alexandra was hurting too badly to notice much. She thanked Mr. and Mrs. Hughes and allowed a slave to carry her inside and deposit her in the bedroom she was to use. Someone was summoned to wrap her ankle in bandages while someone else helped her undress and found a gown for her to sleep in. The pampering was a luxury she had not experienced since Papa's "indiscretion." Perhaps things were finally beginning to change back to what they should be.

As she drifted into slumber, a voice seemed to whisper in her mind. It didn't speak in words but in warmth. She felt loved.

A thought of her own drifted through and brought her crashing back into wakefulness. Was it a coincidence that Judah Hughes and his servant had found her right after she had pleaded for help from God? Or had the Almighty answered her prayer?

five

Jeremiah finished dressing, picked up his Bible, and headed downstairs to break his fast. He was not surprised to find he was the first to rise. He'd had trouble sleeping, although he could not fault the feather mattress or cotton quilts his hosts had provided. No, it was the prickling of his conscience that had awakened him several times. Finding that the slaves were still preparing food, he decided to go outside and read from his Bible. Delving into the Word should help restore his peace of mind.

The morning was crisp and quite cool, not surprising since the end of the year was drawing close. He drank in the view of the river afforded by the wide porch, which faced in a westerly direction. Having met Judah in New Orleans, he'd had no idea his friend's home would be so breathtaking. It made him think of his dream home, the one he'd described to his uncle in the weeks prior to his departure, the one he hoped to build for the sake of orphaned children.

The river wound around the base of the bluff on which Magnolia Plantation stood, its waters as brown as a cup of chicory coffee. He could see no sign of civilization to the north or to the south. The opposite bank of the river was lowland swamp. To his right stood a dense pine forest, its tree trunks nearly as wide as he was tall. To his left were the cotton fields, acre after acre of white-studded plants that looked ready for the harvest.

When he'd arrived the evening before, he had barely been able to make out the vast cropland Judah and his wife grew. Susannah had told them a halting story of the past months while her husband had been convalescing in New Orleans. He had left her with a competent overseer, never realizing he would be away from home for more than a year.

The overseer had taken a new job a few weeks earlier, leaving Susannah without a man to help her supervise and direct the harvest. Some of their neighbors had leant assistance, but the result was not the same. Many of the fields had not been tended as they should have been. She had held out hope that the return of her husband would turn things around, but without an excellent yield from their cotton fields, they might not be able to meet their obligations. Seed had been purchased on credit last spring; the slaves needed clothing, shelter, and food; and the territorial government had recently sent a notice of taxes due.

A sense of purpose lifted Jeremiah's chin. He believed God had put him in this place for a specific reason. To help his friends regain their prosperity? Maybe. Yet he had promised his uncle that he would establish a trading office in Natchez. How could he possibly accomplish both?

It would be nice to have someone to talk to, someone with whom he could be completely honest, someone who would help him see which path he should take. A vision of a bedraggled beauty danced through his mind. The damsel in distress? He had the feeling she had been pampered and spoiled all of her life. Even though she had been tired and dirty, her demeanor had reminded him of the simpering, self-centered debutantes to be found throughout the upper echelons of New Orleans society—empty-minded adornments purchased by wealthy dandies to produce heirs and embellish their elegant homes. Although he had never had the time or desire to attend fancy balls or court rich heiresses, he knew better than to think he could ever bare his soul to such as the woman he had rescued last night.

Yet if he closed his eyes, he could smell the lemony fragrance of her perfume. He could almost feel her in his arms. Her face had been streaked with dirt and mud, but it had still been beautiful. A grin lit his features as he remembered how she had cast him in the role of a cheeky servant. Somehow, he had failed to correct her. No matter, he would probably never see her again.

Jeremiah spied a wooden bench at the edge of the pine forest and headed for it. Brushing it free of pine needles, he sat down. He closed his eyes for a moment and prayed for the wisdom to make good decisions in the days ahead. He thanked God for forgiveness and asked for the grace to forgive others. Pledging his love, utter and complete, to his Maker, Jeremiah felt a sense of peace settle over him, and he sat still, caught up in wonder.

He opened his eyes and realized his Bible had fallen open while he prayed. The book of the prophet Jeremiah, his namesake. His eyes went straight to an underlined verse in chapter 29: *"For I know the thoughts that I think toward you, saith the Lord, thoughts of peace, and not of evil, to give you an expected end."* It was one of his favorite verses. The assurance that God sent His thoughts into Jeremiah's heart brought him great comfort. All he needed to do was be willing to follow God's lead. Everything else would follow in due course. He whispered his thanks to the Lord for the reminder. It settled his mind and gave him the strength to face whatever challenges might come his way. How could he have forgotten this truth?

A noise behind him indicated the other residents of the Hughes household were no longer abed. He turned to see Judah leaning against his crutches, standing in nearly the same spot Jeremiah had stood earlier. How would he adapt to the demands of running Magnolia Plantation? Would he and Susannah lose their home? Judah had told him it was an inheritance from a distant uncle. While Judah had never expected to be a planter, he had managed in the past. Now with only one good leg, would he be able to cope? Only time would tell.

Jeremiah pushed himself up from his bench and strode toward the porch. "You look very natural standing there."

"I don't know. Sometimes I think God is trying to tell me He intends something different for my life." Judah turned a troubled expression toward him. "There's so much to do. How can I—"

"That may be why I am here."

"Thank you, friend, but I cannot impose on your good nature. Both of us know why you're here."

"Have I ever told you how much I have always wanted to be a farmer?"

Judah's face registered his surprise. "You. . .a farmer? I don't believe it." He laughed and shook his head.

"I believe I'm offended." Jeremiah raised his eyebrows. "Do you think me incapable?"

"No, no." Judah lifted one of his crutches and pressed it against the banister that ringed his porch. "But I won't let you sacrifice your uncle's business for mine."

"I have been thinking about that, and I may have a solution."

"What do you mean?" Judah returned his crutch to the floor and leaned against it.

"I still have several things to work out before I present my idea to you. I only brought it up so you will not lose hope. In the meantime"—Jeremiah waggled his eyebrows—"I plan to roll up my sleeves and learn about your farming operation from the ground up."

Judah groaned. "What a clown."

"I know. I know." Jeremiah walked to the front door and held it open for his friend. "A wonderful aroma is emanating from your dining room. Shall we investigate its source?"

six

Alexandra rested her weight on her foot with care, breathing a sigh of relief that the pain from last night had faded considerably. "The salve you put on my ankle has worked, Jemma."

"Yes, ma'am." The sparkle in Jemma's eyes bespoke her pleasure. "One of the grooms gave it to me."

"A groom?" A mental picture of a horse with a pulled fetlock entered her mind.

"After you were carried inside last night."

Heat bloomed in Alexandra's cheeks as she recalled being held so close to a man's chest that the thumping of his heart was all she could hear. Whatever was wrong with her? Was she daydreaming of a servant? Her mind must be addled by all the alarms and grief she had faced recently. She put a hand on her forehead but could not detect any fever. Perhaps she needed more rest.

Jemma flung open the velvet drapes that covered her bedroom window, and sunlight flooded the room.

The day was more advanced than Alexandra had realized. With a sigh, she put away the idea of returning to the refuge of her bed. Grand-mère was probably irritated already because she was not present at the breakfast table.

Jemma helped Alexandra exchange her sleeping gown for a day dress, which had been aired and pressed sometime after their arrival last night. It was black, of course, as befitted a grieving daughter, but the bodice clung to her figure almost like a second skin. Looking in the mirror as Jemma arranged her hair, Alexandra decided the dark material of her skirt contrasted nicely with the white skin of her chest and arms. Of course she was not on the lookout for a suitor since her heart had so recently been broken, but it was always better to be prepared for any circumstance.

She sallied forth from her bedroom some time later and negotiated the central staircase with caution. The dining hall was toward the rear of the house, closer to the kitchen out back. She entered the room, not surprised to see that everyone was still seated at the table. Alexandra put on her widest smile and bent to kiss the wrinkled face of Althea Tanner, her grandmother. "How nice it is to be home."

Grand-mère frowned as she turned her cheek up for Alexandra's kiss, her faded brown eyes as hard as acorns. "I'm not certain when *my* home became a sanctuary for wayward females."

Alexandra spotted her mother seated at the far end of the table, a further indication of Grand-mère's displeasure. The empty plate next to Mama was a sure sign of where she was to sit, so Alexandra moved in that direction, limping ever so slightly in an attempt to remind the others that she was not well.

Uncle John, as tall and thin as ever, stood and held her chair out for her. "It is good to see you, niece."

Her smile warmed. "Thank you, Uncle John." She hugged him before sliding into her chair.

Her mother reached for her hand under the table and squeezed it tightly. It was a warning to mind her tongue.

Alexandra returned the squeeze as her gaze roamed over the assembled family members. Aunt Patricia, Mama's older sister, was almost as tall and thin as her husband. Her smile, as kind and gentle as ever, reminded Alexandra that her aunt was the most charitable member of the Tanner family. Opposite Alexandra sat her cousin, Percival, Grand-mère's nephew who had lived with her since the death of his parents many years ago.

"Now that you are here"—Grand-mère's voice drew Alexandra's attention—"I will tell you the same thing I have been saying to your mother. I will not tolerate an indefinite stay." She pointed a gnarled finger at Alexandra. "You will find a husband. And I don't mean you will wait on the front porch for some suitor to appear. I sent untold amounts of money to your parents to make certain you would turn into an accomplished young lady."

"And we did as you instructed with your money." Mama showed an uncharacteristic willingness to challenge her strong-willed parent. "If you had been as willing to support James's aspirations, we would not be in this fix now."

"Don't you dare try to lay your husband's misdeeds at my door, Beatrice. Although I don't fault him for trying to take advantage of whatever situation arose, he should not have been caught. His actions severely limit your own daughter's prospects."

Having handily subdued her daughter, Grand-mère turned her attention to Alexandra once again. "You have been allowed to dillydally around for far too long. If you don't marry soon, you will be considered an old maid. And then there is the matter of your father's death. As soon as folks around here learn about the scandal surrounding my daughter's husband, they will think twice about letting their sons court you. I refuse to let you squander your chances to have a household of your own."

Alexandra's mouth dropped open. She had always known she would have to marry one day. In fact, she was looking forward to having a household of her own. But to be ordered to marry right away? Preposterous. She closed her mouth with a snap. "I suppose you have a candidate in mind. . ."

"As a matter of fact, I do."

Alexandra should not have been surprised. Grand-mère had probably been planning this since she and Mama had first written of their troubles. She had always pushed Alexandra toward the accomplishments that would assure her granddaughter's place in society, one of station and wealth. "Have I met this paragon?"

Grand-mère's eyes narrowed at the irony in Alexandra's

tone. "Yes, he is Harvey and Marie Sheffield's oldest son. A fine catch. All the girls in the area are chasing him. You will have to work hard if you are to snare him."

Alexandra's lips folded into a straight line. She didn't like being told what to do. "You know the people here will want to know how Papa died. How do you suggest we suppress the truth?"

"I've thought of that, too." Her grandmother sat back in her chair and lifted a hand. The slave who had been standing in one corner of the dining room moved forward at the signal and pulled back the heavy chair on which she sat. Grandmère grabbed the slave's arm and pulled herself upright, grabbing her cane for support. "We'll tell everyone your father died fighting Indians. We'll make sure they believe he was a hero."

Alexandra pushed back her untouched breakfast. Her stomach was roiling. Lie to everyone? Yet what choice did she have? Her grandmother's commands were not to be ignored. She controlled everyone in the family.

In that instant, Alexandra made up her mind. "Once we renew our acquaintance, Mr. Sheffield will not notice anyone else."

❧

Alexandra had the chance to prove her words faster than she had imagined. Grand-mère sent Uncle John and Aunt Patricia to the Sheffield home with a personal invitation to join them for dinner that evening to welcome Alexandra and her mother back home. Since the invitation was closer to a command, the Sheffields accepted and pledged they would bring their son along to renew his acquaintance with the ladies.

Alexandra had Jemma ready her fanciest dress, black of course, but its bodice was outlined with wispy black lace, and tiny gray rosettes were scattered across the slim skirt. It was a dress she would feel comfortable wearing to the fanciest ball in either Nashville or New Orleans. The only danger was appearing overdressed for a simple dinner, but she wanted to impress Mr. Sheffield from the start, and appearance was at least half the battle.

Jemma used an iron on her dark hair, coaxing it into a cascade of ringlets that outlined Alexandra's face, highlighting her cheekbones and making her appear sophisticated. A touch of citrus perfume dabbed at her wrists completed the toilette. Alexandra slipped the ribbon of her black lace fan around her wrist and glanced in the mirror to judge the impact. She looked awfully somber.

"Just think how nice it will be to have your own household," she lectured herself. "And how bad it will be if Grandmère throws you out." She took a deep breath and practiced a wide smile. Much better. Lowell Sheffield would be bowled over.

The guests were already assembled in the front parlor when Alexandra made her grand entrance. She paused for a moment at the wide doorway to the room.

"Well, come in here, girl." Grand-mère waved her cane. "We've been waiting for your arrival for nigh on an hour."

Not the best introduction, but Alexandra made certain her smile did not falter. "Please forgive me." The men stood as she entered. Sweeping past everyone else, she bent over her grandmother and kissed the air next to the old woman's cheek.

"Humph." Her grandmother glared at her. "I suppose we'll survive." She turned to Mr. and Mrs. Sheffield. "This saucy thing is, of course, my granddaughter Alexandra."

"You've become quite the beauty, bound to turn our local girls green with envy." Harvey Sheffield was a barrel-chested man with a forehead that seemed inordinately high, likely an illusion caused by his receding hairline.

Marie Sheffield, as slender as her husband was wide, nodded from her seat on the sofa. "Yes, indeed. And the young men will buzz around her like bees in a flower garden."

Alexandra curtsied with all the grace she could muster and

tried not to stare at the light reflecting from Mr. Sheffield's nearly bare pate. "You are too kind."

"My parents speak nothing but the truth." The man whom her grandmother had picked to become Alexandra's husband moved toward her, one hand covering his heart while the other reached for her hand. "I can hardly believe how stunning you've become since the last time I saw you." He bowed in front of her and placed a warm kiss on her wrist.

Her heart fluttered at the audacious move and warmth spread upward, burning her cheeks and ears. She pulled her hand from his and spread the ribs of her fan, using it to cool her face. "You have also changed since we were children, Mr. Sheffield."

Lowell Sheffield had filled out well in the intervening years. His naturally curly brown hair was pulled forward from the crown and framed his wide forehead in a most attractive manner. His shoulders, which she remembered as being rather narrow, had widened, and his chest was at least as deep as his father's. All in all, he was a passably attractive specimen. Becoming his wife would not be as dreadful as she had feared.

"I hope you are as pleased with my transformation as I am with yours, Miss Lewis."

His smile was handsome, too. Alexandra could understand why he was so popular with the single ladies. It had probably made him a bit overconfident. She used her fan to obscure the lower part of her face and studied him from head to toe. She took her time, as though she was uncertain of the answer she should give. After a moment, his smile wilted. Hers widened, but he could not see it because of the fan.

Alexandra bit her lip and lowered the fan. "Yes. . .of course you do." She put enough emphasis on the words to imply the opposite. Then she turned and sat next to his mother, complimenting the lady on her hair and dress. She listened with one ear as Mrs. Sheffield described in tedious detail the process of obtaining a seamstress who could copy patterns properly.

Alexandra's heart was beating like a kettledrum. Had her ploy worked? Only time would tell. She nodded at the appropriate places and eventually drew Mr. Sheffield, Lowell's father, into the conversation. By the time dinner was announced, she had at least two fervent supporters.

As soon as she stood, Lowell was at her side, his arm held out in invitation.

Alexandra put on her most innocent air and looked past him. "Grand-mère, do you have anyone to help you to the dinner table?"

Her grandmother snorted. "Your uncle will see to me. Go on with your young man."

With what she hoped was a convincing start, Alexandra turned to Lowell Sheffield. "Oh my, where did you come from?"

"I think you are toying with me, Miss Lewis." He offered his arm once again, a quizzical expression on his face. His eyes were a deep hazel color, reminding her of a shady woodland.

She put her hand on his arm, widening her eyes as she gazed up at him. "Me, sir? I am naught but a poor country girl. What makes you think I would dare tease someone as debonair as you, Mr. Sheffield?"

He smiled down at her as he led her to the dining room. "Because I don't believe you are blind."

Alexandra could not suppress the giggle that rose to her throat. Her heart fluttered once again as she caught his hazel gaze. His laughter mingled with hers, and they entered the dining room on an intimate note. It seemed Mr. Sheffield enjoyed a challenge. She would have to make certain she gave him one.

The only empty seats at the table, except for Grand-mère's and Uncle John's, were side by side. She wished her family had not made it quite so obvious they were throwing her at Lowell's head. It would have been smarter for someone to have arranged the table so that the two of them sat across from each other. Then he would have a front row seat for her bubbly personality. She could have flirted shamelessly with the elder Mr. Sheffield, further piquing the younger Mr. Sheffield's interest. But she would have to work with what she had been given.

During the first course, she was very attentive to her mother, who sat on her right. Mr. Sheffield was thus forced to converse with Cousin Percival, who always had more interest in his dinner than in dinner conversation.

"You cannot ignore me any longer," his breath whispered in her ear. "Etiquette demands that you converse with me a little."

Alexandra turned her head in his direction. He was leaning so close to her that their mouths nearly touched. Her gaze fastened on his lips. "I. . .I. . ." She forced herself to look up into his eyes. The specks of green in them seemed to have caught fire. Lowell Sheffield was definitely interested. And her tongue seemed to be stuck to the roof of her mouth.

Grand-mère cleared her throat, snapping the thread that seemed to have bound both of them. "Have you visited with the Hugheses to thank them for rescuing you and your mother?"

"Rescue?" Lowell sat back in his chair, but his eyes still seemed to devour Alexandra's face. "What happened that you needed to be rescued?"

Her mind whirled as she recounted the story of their arrival and her sprained ankle. She was pleased to have so easily secured Lowell's interest, but she wondered if her actions had started a fire that would scorch her. Yet the admiration in his gaze made her feel good. She and Mama had been social outcasts before their departure. It was wonderful to return to the status she had once enjoyed.

"If you could wait until the afternoon, I would be happy to escort you to Magnolia Plantation." Lowell's offer pierced her tumultuous thoughts.

She turned to her grandmother for permission, even though

she knew it was a foregone conclusion.

"Of course you may go." Her grandmother's smile embraced everyone at the table. "I am very appreciative Mr. Sheffield can take time out of his busy day to escort you. Such a strong young man will be able to protect you no matter what may occur."

"It's all settled then." Lowell's shoulders had straightened at her grandmother's complimentary words. "I look forward to spending more time with you."

Alexandra's heart sped up at the look in his eyes. She had little doubt she would wring a proposal from this man in less than two weeks.

seven

"But I love you." Susannah moved from her chair by the window and sat down next to her husband.

Jeremiah turned his head and wondered if he could get outside without drawing the attention of Judah and his wife. This conversation was much too personal for him to witness. And part of him wanted to chastise Judah again for focusing on his disability. God had given him so many blessings—not the least of which were a Christian wife who loved him dearly, a beautiful home, and the chance to fulfill whatever God's plan was for him. If only he would let himself see the truth.

"We're embarrassing our guest." Judah looked at Jeremiah, a martyred expression on his face. His cheeks were red with mortification, and his fingers plucked at the material of the sofa on which he sat.

His wife was sitting next to him, determination apparent in the tilt of her chin and the straight line of her shoulders. "Are you so proud you cannot listen to reason?"

Judah sighed and shook his head. "You and I can discuss this later. For now, we need to think about what is necessary for the plantation. We need someone to oversee the slaves."

"But the slave you selected to act as the overseer's captain, Oren, has been working as hard as he can to get the other slaves working." Susannah slid to the far end of the sofa and crossed her arms. "It's true he is not as effective as an overseer, but we have managed to get a few things done since Mr. Heidel left."

Jeremiah took a deep breath, glad he had not slinked away a few moments earlier. He had the answer if the two of them would only listen to reason. "I can do the work."

"That's out of the question." Judah's frown centered on him. "You're a guest here. I'm already beholden to you for bringing me home. I couldn't ask you to take on the responsibilities of an overseer."

"I didn't hear you asking me." Jeremiah leaned against the mantel and watched his friend. "I want to do this."

Susannah looked up at him, her eyes large and moist as if she was holding back tears. "We can't afford to pay you much."

Jeremiah held up a hand to stop her. "If you can put up with my ugly face for the next few months, that will be payment enough."

Sputtering laughter came from Judah. He looked at his wife, who nodded. "If you're serious. . ."

Jeremiah straightened and stepped toward the sofa. "I won't let you down."

"There's no doubt about that." Susannah reached for her husband's hand across the space she had put between them. "You've been an answer to our prayers."

"Where can I find this Oren you mentioned?"

Judah wrapped his large fingers around his wife's hand, pulling her toward him. "He'll probably be in the south field today."

Jeremiah nodded. "I'll be back before sunset."

"You'd better be back in time for tea." The loving glance Susannah had given her husband turned into resolve as she raised her chin and glared at Jeremiah. "I don't want to have to come get you from the fields."

"Yes, ma'am." Jeremiah rolled up his sleeves and headed out the door. "I'll see you for tea."

He strode across the front lawn, passing several out-buildings that had different functions. He recognized the grist mill, smokehouse, kitchen, and barns, but he made a mental note to investigate the other buildings. He arrived at the south field as the sun was reaching its zenith.

Oren, a tall, muscular black man, was directing the workers

in the field, but to Jeremiah's eyes, little actual work was being done. Only a handful of men were trailing long sacks partially filled with white cotton bolls. The rest of the slaves were sitting or lying on the ground and watching.

"Oren!" As soon as Jeremiah called out the slave's name, a furor arose. The slaves who had been lolling about jumped to their feet and grabbed their cotton sacks. The ones who had been working stopped and gaped at him.

Oren walked toward him, a look of fear on his face.

Jeremiah held out his hand. "I understand you've been doing your best to get the crops in."

"Yessir." The slave looked at his outstretched hand and then back at Jeremiah's face. He didn't offer his hand. "Has Missus Hughes hired you to take over?"

"Not exactly." Jeremiah realized the man was too scared to shake his hand. He should have realized things would not be the same as they were in New Orleans. Although many people in his hometown owned slaves, many free blacks also lived there. But this man had probably never dreamed of such a world. "I am a friend of the family, and I hope to work with you and the others to make sure we catch up on the harvest."

The slave beamed at him. "I sure is glad yore here, sir."

"My name is Jeremiah."

"Yessir, Master Jeremiah."

"Just plain Jeremiah will do, Oren. I'm not your master. I don't know much about picking cotton, but I'm willing to work beside the men here. Is there a sack I can use?"

Oren's smile slipped, puzzlement plain on his face. "You want to work?"

"That's right. I believe in laboring alongside those who work for me." He looked toward the fields where all the hands had stopped. "So who's going to show me what y'all spend all your time doing?"

It didn't take the slaves long to realize Jeremiah was serious. He was given a sack and shown how to wear the long strap that was used to drag it behind him. He watched with curiosity as Oren showed him how to separate the fluffy cotton from its prickly casing.

After an hour in the sun, Jeremiah was hot, and his back was aching. He could not imagine how hard this work would be in the heat of summer and early autumn.

The other men avoided him, whispering to each other as they worked. To take his mind off his discomforts, Jeremiah began to hum his favorite song, "Love Divine, All Loves Excelling," breaking into words as he got to the final verse. He reached the end of a row and turned, starting his hymn all over again. This time he sang all the words, letting his voice broaden as spiritual joy filled him.

He didn't notice when another voice joined his, but soon, many voices were singing praises to God. He straightened and looked around him, humbled by the realization that these slaves knew Charles Wesley's hymn as well as he did. It was further proof that they were all God's children. In that moment, he knew he would have to do something to ease the burden of slavery until he could convince Judah and Susannah to free their slaves.

eight

"How do you expect me to captivate someone as handsome and interesting as Lowell Sheffield when I am limited to wearing nothing but black?" Alexandra twirled around, her skirts swirling with her. Her dress was cut in the newest style—empire waist, narrow skirt, and short sleeves—but the black cloth was only relieved by a narrow collar of lavender lace.

Her mother's eyebrows crowded together. "You can't flaunt tradition by abandoning your mourning colors so soon after your father's death. We will both have to dress in black for at least a year."

Alexandra collapsed on her bed. She put a hand under her chin and considered. "But it's not like we're living in Philadelphia or Boston. It's not even New Orleans. And you know how many compliments I receive from gentlemen when I wear brighter colors."

"I don't know, dear. . . ."

Part of Alexandra wished her mother would argue with her instead of sitting there, staring off into the distance. If only Papa had not—

She shook her head to clear it of the useless thought. Papa *had*, and the past could not be changed. The color of her dress seemed unimportant compared to the path she and her mother were being forced to take. "Come on, Mama. Let's go downstairs. It's too late to change, anyway. Mr. Sheffield will be here any moment."

Alexandra's gaze followed her mother's as it wandered around the room that had always been her special haven during visits. The pastel colors of the draperies and spread had faded a little over the years, but they brought her a sense of comfort nevertheless. To round out Alexandra's education, Grand-mère had paid for an expensive teacher to come from New Orleans and instruct her in the art of watercolors. If her family was to be believed, she had some talent, so her landscapes were framed and hung in the room. Now they served as an ever-present reminder of happier times.

A knock on the door was followed by Jemma's voice. "You have a guest in the parlor, Miss Alexandra."

"Thank you." Alexandra bent over her mother and pressed a kiss on her cheek. "Are you coming downstairs?"

Mama patted her cheek. "Of course I'll come downstairs." She gathered her shawl and pulled it around her shoulders before drifting toward the door.

Mr. Sheffield whisked Alexandra out of the house in a matter of minutes, ushering her into his carriage with a flourish. It was a fancy vehicle with large wheels and a plush seat perched high above the ground. "I hope you are not afraid of my phaeton."

"Not at all." Alexandra looked out over the landscape, savoring the wide view. "I love the feeling of wind rushing past."

"You are so different than most of the girls around here." He picked up the reins and guided the horse toward the main road. "Eager to enjoy whatever comes your way."

Alexandra cast an admiring glance in his direction. "And you are a very astute man." She placed a gloved hand on his arm. "But I'm sure you hear that every day, Mr. Sheffield."

His ardent glance nearly scorched her. "I wish you would call me Lowell. All my closest acquaintants do."

Wondering if things might be progressing a little too fast, Alexandra removed her hand and shifted a few inches away from him. "We aren't children any longer."

"No, Alexandra, but I am beginning to think we may be destined for something more lasting than a childhood friendship."

She wasn't sure if it was the flirtatious tone of his voice, the usage of her first name, or the heady feeling of thundering across the countryside, but her heart seemed to be galloping faster than the horse in front of them.

The road was far enough from Natchez and the Mississippi River that they saw few other travelers, only rolling fields of hay, corn, or cotton. When they turned off the main road, she was surprised to see field after field of unpicked cotton. She had been in the area for less than a week, but the Hugheses seemed to be behind on their harvest. Grand-mère's fields were barren in comparison.

The carriage turned around a bend in the road, and she spotted a group of slaves who were working on the far side of a cotton field. She raised a hand to shade her gaze and realized a white man was working with the slaves. Alexandra frowned. She'd never seen an overseer who labored alongside the slaves. Was that why the Hugheses were so far behind their neighbors?

As if her gaze had disturbed the man, he straightened and stared in her direction. He looked familiar, but with the distance separating them, she could not recall where she might have seen him before. Then they were past the field, turning into the tree-shaded drive that led to the Hughes plantation home, and Alexandra pushed the thought away.

The Hughes plantation was impressive, although not as large as her grandmother's home. The two-story building had a deep porch running across the front, topped by a balcony that was equally long and deep. Old oaks shadowed a pond on one side of the front lawn. Alexandra spotted a white egret standing on the bank, watching the dark water, undisturbed by their arrival.

A slave ran toward them and grabbed their horse's halter. Lowell climbed down and tossed the reins to the boy before walking around to assist her.

Alexandra placed her slippered foot on the wooden step for dismounting and leaned forward into Lowell's raised hands. He swung her toward the ground with ease and set her on her feet. She thought of stumbling on purpose so he would have to catch her but decided at the last moment to step back. Sometimes it was good to be a little unattainable. "Thank you."

He raised an eyebrow, tucked his chin, and stared at her.

"Thank you. . .Lowell."

His smile was as attractive as any she'd ever seen. "It's my pleasure."

She brought up her parasol and opened it to protect her complexion from the autumn sunlight. The action also gave her time to quiet the butterflies fluttering in her stomach. Lowell was going to make a superb husband. Rich enough to grant her every wish and exciting enough to make any girl's heart trip. Alexandra had to admit her grandmother had chosen the perfect man for her.

A slave ushered them into the wide entry hall common to most plantation homes. Several doors opened onto this area, and the slave led them toward one on the right. Lowell gave her both of their names so the slave could announce their arrival to Judah and Susannah Hughes.

The room they entered was somewhat smaller than her grandmother's formal parlor, but it felt. . .cozy. The worn sofa on which Judah and his wife sat looked comfortable, if not fashionable. A scuffed, round table stood in front of it, a gleaming silver service atop it. On the far side of the table, three straight-backed chairs crowded each other, providing a place for guests to sit. Sheer curtains billowed around the tall, open windows. The breeze that moved them brushed her cheeks.

Mr. Hughes was struggling to get his crutches under his arm.

Alexandra's heart went out to him. "Please don't rise on my account, sir."

"Nonsense." He smiled at her as he pulled himself up. "What kind of man does not observe basic etiquette? Especially when visited by such a beautiful young lady."

His wife rose, too. "It's so nice to see you, Miss Lewis, Mr.

Sheffield. Welcome to our home."

"Thank you." Alexandra curtsied to both of them before sinking into one of the chairs.

Mrs. Hughes sat back down, waiting until both of the gentlemen had also taken their seats. "How is your foot?"

"I am fully recovered, thanks to your kindness in rescuing me."

Mr. Hughes shook his head. "All we did was offer a ride. It was Jeremiah who rescued you."

Alexandra was about to answer him when the door to the parlor opened once more. She turned to see the subject of her host's pronouncement enter. Of course! He was the man she had just seen across the cotton fields. No wonder he looked so familiar. But what was he doing in the parlor? Did he have some message for his master?

He had apparently taken a moment to rinse his face, although his cheekbones were flushed from his time in the bright sunlight. His sleeves were rolled up to his elbows, and her gaze seemed caught by the muscles in his lower arms. Her mind flashed to the first night she'd seen him. She could almost feel those strong arms supporting her shoulders and knees.

The butterflies Lowell had caused earlier became more insistent, beating against her chest as though trying to escape. What had happened to the breeze? The air seemed to have been sucked out as this Jeremiah entered the room.

"Jeremiah." Susannah raised a hand and the servant bowed over it. "We were just speaking of you."

The butterflies got caught in Alexandra's throat as the man turned his blue gaze in her direction. Unable to speak, she nodded at him, expecting him to turn from her and give some note or information to Mr. Hughes.

But he didn't. Instead he seated himself in the chair next to hers. Whatever was the world coming to when a servant sat down to partake of tea? Her shocked gaze swept from him to the Hugheses. Neither of them looked as though anything was out of place.

"Miss Lewis, isn't it? Are you and your mother recovered from your journey?" His voice curled around her, setting the butterflies loose once more.

Before Alexandra could voice her astonishment at his breach of manners, Mr. Hughes leaned forward. "That's right. The two of you have not even been properly introduced. Miss Lewis, please allow me to introduce Jeremiah LeGrand, a man who has proven himself to be a courageous and devoted friend."

As Mr. Hughes continued the introduction, Alexandra pinned a fake smile on her lips. She didn't care if the man had single-handedly defeated the whole British Navy; he was a servant. He must be taking advantage of his master's gratitude to insinuate himself into the society of his betters. It should not be allowed. She drew away from him, practically moving into Lowell's lap. Not that the latter would mind.

She wished Mr. and Mrs. Hughes had not put her in this position. She wished she had not twisted her foot in Natchez Under-the-Hill. She wished this Jeremiah LeGrand had not helped her. Or that Grand-mère had sent someone to meet them. Only one of those little details would have made this afternoon unnecessary.

"Mr. . . .LeGrand. You seem to be in the habit of rescuing others. Is that why you were working in the fields a little while ago?" She wondered if anyone else in the room noticed the frost in her voice. A quick glance at Mr. LeGrand's stiff features gave her the answer. If he wanted to push his way into higher society, he would need to develop thicker skin.

"I try to follow the Lord's bidding." His voice didn't sound angry, but she felt the sting of his words.

She lifted her chin and shot him an angry glance. "As do all good Christians."

"Would you care for tea, Miss Lewis?" Susannah Hughes's voice interrupted the staring contest between them.

Alexandra turned to her hostess and nodded, accepting the china being offered. She balanced the delicate saucer on her knee and sipped from the matching cup.

Mrs. Hughes served tea to the others in the room and the conversation became more general.

Lowell was the perfect gentleman, answering questions about his parents and sharing amusing anecdotes of local parties and hostesses. Then he coughed and leaned forward. "I regret my parents would not allow me to join you fellows in New Orleans. I would have enjoyed fighting next to Old Hickory."

The man on the other side of her grimaced. "I thought General Jackson had an impossible task, but God stepped in."

"What do you mean?" Alexandra couldn't stay out of the conversation. "I was in New Orleans. General Jackson was nothing short of brilliant. My papa said he was everywhere, tireless even though he was not well."

Judah Hughes put his teacup on the table in front of him. "I don't think Jeremiah would disagree with you, would you?" He waited until Jeremiah nodded before continuing. "Very few people would dare disparage the Hero of New Orleans."

The smile that turned up the corners of her mouth was so brittle she was surprised it did not shatter. "In that case I apologize, Mr. LeGrand." She also placed her teacup on the table, glancing at Lowell as she did so.

He followed suit, standing and holding a hand out to her. "I believe we should take our leave, Miss Lewis. We have taken up too much of the Hugheses' time."

Alexandra stood up and put her hand on his arm. The other two men stood up, too.

Susannah reached for the bell pull. "It was so kind of you to come and see us. I hope you will visit again soon."

"And you must come to Tanner Plantation. Grand-mère mentioned it specifically when I told her my destination. She said you have not been to visit in quite some time."

"Yes, I have been rather busy, what with the harvest and then the arrival of my wonderful husband." Susannah glanced toward him, her love written plainly across her face.

For a moment, Alexandra was jealous of the woman. As handsome as Lowell was, she could not see herself experiencing the kind of devotion Susannah felt for Judah. Then she caught herself. This poor woman was tied to a cripple, a man who would always struggle to climb stairs, a husband who could never again partner her at a ball. It was a tragedy. Susannah was a woman to be pitied, not envied.

Judah smiled at his wife. "Now that things are returning to normal, I'm certain we can arrange for you to spend some time visiting families here. If we can keep Jeremiah out of the fields, all three of us can go."

"I doubt I'll have much time for that."

A shiver ran up Alexandra's spine as his deep growl sounded behind her. "What a shame." She swung around wondering what game he might be playing now. "I'm surprised you do not see the advantage of being introduced to my family. But perhaps as a servant, you are not aware they are some of the most prominent people in the territory."

Susannah gasped at her words. "What?"

Jeremiah's gaze narrowed on Alexandra's face. "Don't tell me you still think I'm a servant?"

Alexandra could feel the blush starting somewhere in the vicinity of her heart. It rose with all the insistence of an incoming tide, heating her face and ears as if someone was holding a hot iron to them. "What do you mean?"

Judah moved awkwardly toward her. "Jeremiah is not a servant. His uncle is one of the wealthiest men in the country. He has no need of any acquaintance to make his way in our society, here or anywhere else for that matter."

She closed her eyes for a moment and wished the floor would swallow her up. But then her anger turned against the man who had deceived her. Why had he let it go this far? He knew, but he said nothing. Now she would have to apologize. "I am sorry, Mr. LeGrand."

"It's my fault." His blue eyes, so lacking in condemnation, eased her shame. "I should have told you the truth on the night we first met." He shrugged. "But you seemed to have so many more important issues to deal with that evening, and I didn't think I'd ever see you again."

Alexandra was as embarrassed as the day she had discovered she was being shunned by Nashville's elite because of her father's actions. She was relieved when Lowell offered his arm, but she could feel Jeremiah's blue gaze piercing the back of her neck as she was escorted out of the house and long after they had left the Hugheses' land.

The ride home was quiet. She supposed that was her fault. She couldn't think of much to say. Her mind was spinning from the implications of what she had learned. What kind of man worked when he did not have to? What kind of man had so little concern for his reputation that he would allow her to continue misjudging him? She could make no sense of it. Jeremiah was not like any other man she'd ever met.

She filed away her questions for consideration later and turned her attention to Lowell. Perhaps he would appreciate her reticence. He was probably much more used to women who gushed, giggled, and prattled endlessly.

They had almost arrived at her home before she thought to compliment his driving skills. "You are very kind to spend your afternoon squiring me around."

His gaze was so different from the irritating man they had left at the Hughes plantation. His brown eyes were warm, kind, and intelligent. Although there had been warmth in Mr. LeGrand's eyes, they held none of the eagerness she saw in Lowell's. "Spending time with you is quite pleasant."

The words were spoken with as much ardency as she could wish. But where were the butterflies? Had her time in Mr. LeGrand's presence killed the budding romance? Nonsense. All she had to do was concentrate, and they would return. Wouldn't they?

nine

Facing a disapproving relative was not one of Alexandra's favorite pastimes. But it seemed that was what her life had been reduced to. She raised her chin and stared at her aunt's bunched features.

"You should not go visiting by yourself." Aunt Patricia's high-pitched complaint made Alexandra want to stamp her foot.

"And who would you suggest as an escort? Uncle John? Cousin Percival?" The latter was dozing in one corner of the parlor. He didn't even rouse when she said his name. A fine escort he would be. And her uncle had left before daybreak to accompany a large shipment of cotton to the dock in Natchez. He would not return until after dark.

"Your mother could go with you."

Grand-mère shook her head. "She is upstairs abed. It seems she has a sick headache."

"So you see, no one is available." Alexandra pulled on her gloves. "I will take the gig. It has enough room for me to carry them my painting."

Her aunt was still not satisfied. "I don't see why you cannot wait until tomorrow."

"Leave her alone, Patricia," Grand-mère came to her rescue. "No one can blame her for wanting some younger company. Susannah Hughes is an unexceptionable young woman. Exactly the type of matron she should emulate."

"Thank you, Grand-mère." Alexandra kissed the old woman and made her escape.

It was another beautiful day, with a slight chill to the air to presage colder weather. The warm autumn was much more to her liking than the colder weather of Nashville. Frost would probably not dust the ground before Christmas. Alexandra settled herself in the seat and checked to make certain her gift was secure. She hoped Susannah would like the representation of her home. Alexandra had painted it from memory after her visit, including the oak-shaded pond and attractive home. She had even included the white-feathered egret.

It took her longer to reach the Hugheses' home than when she had ridden with Lowell since she was not as daring a driver as he. And the horse pulling her gig was more content to plod than gallop. But she arrived at last to find Susannah, Mr. Hughes, and the fascinating Mr. LeGrand sitting on the front porch.

Susannah met her at the top of the stairs. "What a pleasure to see you again."

Alexandra removed her hat and gloves and handed them to the slave who stood nearby. "I really should have waited until you returned my call last week, but I have a gift for you and could not wait to bring it."

"What a thoughtful gesture." Judah looked stronger than he had before, rising and putting the crutches under his arms with little trouble. He moved to his wife's side and smiled at Alexandra.

"Yes, indeed." Was that irony she heard in Jeremiah's voice?

A flush entered her cheeks. Did he realize he was the real reason for her visit? She glanced in his direction, caught once more by the bright blue of his eyes. Those eyes had haunted her as she worked on her landscape. She had even outlined the planes of his face in her sketchbook—from his broad forehead to the square edges of his chin—but she had not been able to capture the exact color of his eyes. They seemed to be lit from within, inviting her to fall into their depths.

What was the matter with her? Alexandra shook herself mentally and turned from the man. Susannah was looking at her oddly. Had she missed something? The painting. It was still in her hands. She thrust it toward Susannah.

It took the smaller woman only a moment to unwrap the

artwork. Her mouth formed a large O, and she held it so her husband could see it. "It's beautiful, Alexandra."

"You are very talented." Judah added his praise to that of his wife. He turned to Jeremiah. "Come and see. She has painted our front lawn. She even included the egret."

Jeremiah walked over to them, his gaze moving from the painting to her face. "It's excellent, Miss Lewis. God has graced you with a special gift."

Alexandra's pleasure slipped away. What did God have to do with this? She had worked hard to learn the rudiments of color and perspective. God had not graced her at all. She opened her mouth to answer him, but Susannah forestalled her.

"Let's go inside and decide where it should be displayed."

Judah nodded. "I think we should start in the parlor. I've never liked that portrait of your great-uncle over our fireplace. He seems to watch every move I make."

"That is supposed to be the mark of a master, is it not, Miss Lewis?"

Jeremiah's question caught her off guard. Was she supposed to agree with him and discourage the Hugheses from placing her art in a prominent position? Her landscape would be more fitting than the portrait of some dead, forgotten relative.

"I don't care if it's a masterpiece or not," Judah answered. "I would much rather gaze at this landscape while enjoying my tea."

"I will leave the three of you to decide then." Jeremiah bowed in her general direction. "I have work to see to."

Disappointment shot through Alexandra as she watched him stride away. She laughed at some remark Judah made, but her mind was consumed with thoughts of Jeremiah. What had happened to her ability to attract a man's attention? She seemed doomed to failure where Mr. LeGrand was concerned. He was not interested in her at all. Was it because she had mistaken him for a servant?

As she watched the proud set of his shoulders, she wondered how she ever could have thought him anything other than a gentleman. Would she never learn to look beneath surface appearance? She had been misled by his casual dress and failed to see his intelligence and refinement. Perhaps he would one day forgive her for her mistake. ❧

Jeremiah could hear her laughter as he walked toward the building that housed the cotton gin. Was she laughing at him? And why should the thought disturb him so much? She was nothing to him. He didn't even like the type of woman she represented. Hadn't he read just this morning about the dangers of linking his future with a shallow woman?

The urge to return to his bedchamber and open his Bible was nearly irresistible. He wanted to reacquaint himself with the chapter in Proverbs that described the value of a virtuous woman. Perhaps he could take a few moments during the lunch hour for reading. In the meantime, he needed to focus on the task ahead of him.

During the past week, he had instituted several changes in the way work was accomplished on Judah and Susannah's plantation. The first improvement he had made was to remove the female slaves from the field. They were better suited to work in the smokehouse, gin, sewing room, or kitchens. He had also implemented work breaks for the men in the field. They were allowed two half-hour breaks for eating and several smaller breaks for sitting in the shade and cooling off with water from the nearby stream. The result was a better harvest as the workers were no longer pushed to the limits of their endurance.

Jeremiah entered the wooden building that had been reserved for use in ginning cotton. Judah and Susannah had made the decision to invest in the hand-cranked apparatus when they first came to Magnolia Plantation. He had read about the invention that separated cotton seed from the fiber but had never seen it working until he came here. It still boggled his mind to see how much cotton could be processed in a single day's time. The cleaned fiber was packed into bales for shipment back east, where it would be turned into the strong cloth that seemed to be more in demand with each passing day.

He watched the process for a little while, making certain the machinery was working properly and the slaves inside were not having any problems. Seeing their shy smiles was rewarding. Even though he did not have the power to free them, he could make certain their circumstances were as humane as possible.

After leaving the cotton gin, he poked his head in the sewing room to find a roomful of women sitting in a circle of chairs, their fingers flying as they worked on making everything from tablecloths to shifts and trousers for the slaves. Young girls worked next to the older women, concentrating on making straight stitches with the same speed and skill. He was again reminded of the verses in Proverbs.

God seemed to be tapping him on the shoulder, pushing him to return to the house. He hoped Alexandra would be gone by now, but even if she was still there, perhaps he could avoid seeing her if he was very quiet. He cast a longing glance at the vacant overseer's house as he walked. He had wanted to move into it, but Judah and Susannah would not hear of it. They insisted he stay in the big house with them.

Alexandra's gig was still out front, so Jeremiah circled around to a side entrance. Using the back stairs, he climbed to the second floor. The slave who was sweeping and dusting in his room hurried out as he entered, leaving the door wide open.

Jeremiah found himself stretching his hearing to try and make out what was being discussed in the parlor on the first floor and thought he heard his name. Were they discussing him? Were Susannah and Judah telling her what he was doing with the slaves? Was she impressed with his progressive ideas, or did she think he was being foolhardy? And what did it matter anyway?

Disgusted at the direction of his thoughts, Jeremiah closed

the bedroom door with a snap and turned to his bedside table. The black leather Bible sitting on it drew him. He sat on the edge of his bed and grabbed it, opening it to Proverbs. He found the thirty-first chapter and his finger ran down the page to verse 10: "Who can find a virtuous woman? for her price is far above rubies."

He stopped and considered the words. They still held true today. He had met many women in his lifetime, but most of the ones considered a good match were calculating and manipulative. Alexandra Lewis was a good example. Yet something about her captured his imagination. Perhaps it was her weakness the first time they had met. In spite of her evident pain, Alexandra had been more concerned about her mother and her slave than her own comfort.

He closed his Bible with a sigh and sank to his knees next to the bed. "Lord, You know my heart belongs to You. I am content to remain single if it is Your will, but if not, please lead me to a straightforward and honest woman who loves You with the same love and devotion I feel. A part of me would like someone who loves me in the same way Susannah loves Judah, but that is secondary to living the life You direct." A feeling of peace settled on him. He basked in the privilege of serving God even though he was only a man. "God, thank You for sacrificing Your Son for my sake. For providing the way to eternal life in Your presence. Help me to always keep You first in all my ways. Amen."

He pushed himself up and returned the Bible to its place on the table. It was time to get back outside. He had a lot of work to accomplish before his day was over. His uneasiness banished, Jeremiah felt ready to tackle whatever problems lay ahead.

ten

The Christmas season was especially hard without Papa.

The family continued to follow their holiday traditions. On Christmas Eve, a tree was brought into the parlor. The ladies strung berries to decorate it while Uncle John read the account of Christ's birth from Luke. Alexandra gave each member of the family a miniature she had painted, a project that had kept her busy in the weeks leading to Christmas. So busy she almost didn't notice Lowell's absence...almost.

He had not been back to see her since the day he took her to Magnolia Plantation to visit the Hugheses. Had he heard something? No, that was silly. She had attended a small dinner last week and learned the Sheffields were out of town on business. Surely Lowell would visit once they returned.

Alexandra bid her relatives good night and sought her bedchamber, trying to ignore the pervading gloom. It seemed she could feel the passage of time in her very bones. What would she do if Lowell did not return? Could she find another suitable candidate among the local families? She tried to imagine flirting with some of the men she had met. Would they be as responsive as Lowell? Or would they spurn her efforts with the same haughty attitude Mr. LeGrand had adopted?

She rolled over and punched her pillow as she relived his rejection. How dare he? And why was it his blue gaze followed her into her dreams?

❧

Soft, cold rain pattered against Alexandra's windowsill on Christmas morning. The gray drops drained the countryside of the remnants of color. The grass was hidden under a carpet of brown leaves, and even the green pine needles drooped under the weight of the raindrops. Alexandra felt as sad as they looked. Would she ever experience unadulterated happiness again? Or would her father's death overshadow every joy? She felt broken, lost. And she didn't know where to turn to find herself again.

She walked to the mirror above her washbasin and pointed a finger at the reflection. "You will stop pitying yourself. No man likes a female who cannot brighten his day." She hardly recognized the woman who looked back. Large dark eyes, narrow nose, and wide mouth. Her ebony hair gleamed in the yellow light of a kerosene lamp. With an impatient hand, she twisted it back and pinned it into a hasty knot. Was she beautiful? Most men seemed to think so. But was beauty enough?

She thought of her mother and grandmother who had both been vivacious when they were younger. Her mother, however, seemed to be fading as quickly as the grass outside. And while her grandmother had not faded away, Alexandra wasn't certain she wanted to be as domineering as the matriarch of the family. Was there some way to avoid either future?

She turned from the mirror and grabbed a shawl. Tanner Plantation was draftier than she remembered. She hurried downstairs to the dining room and took her place. Mama drifted in soon after, followed by Aunt Patricia, Uncle John, and Cousin Percival.

Grand-mère entered last, taking her seat at the head of the table. "I have received a note from Mrs. Sheffield."

Grand-mère's announcement caught Alexandra by surprise. She looked up from the plate of coddled eggs and met the older woman's gaze. "She's returned to Natchez?"

"Yes." Grand-mère helped herself to several slices of bacon and a piece of toast. "She will be visiting this afternoon. I expect you to be present."

Alexandra nodded. "Did she say whether Lowell will accompany her?"

"Such a nice young man." The comment came from her

•

mother. "I look forward to renewing our acquaintance."

"She did not say," her grandmother responded before turning to Aunt Patricia. "Will you be here?"

Aunt Patricia shook her head. "You know I always visit the poor on Mondays. I consider it my Christian duty to take care of those who are not as fortunate as you and me." She turned and stared at Alexandra. "I had hoped to convince you to join me today."

Alexandra was relieved to have a valid excuse. She had gone with her aunt a few weeks earlier and found it depressing. They visited families who lived in single-room hovels with dirt floors. The people were grateful for the baskets of herbs, fruits, and vegetables—and Alexandra was grateful to bid them good-bye. She shrugged and made a mental note to have another pressing engagement before Monday rolled around again.

"She will be here with me awaiting our visitors." Grandmère looked back toward Alexandra. "And I trust you will look a great deal more presentable. Whether your young man is present or not, you need to remember to always put forth your best efforts."

Anger flashed through her, but Alexandra pressed her lips together. She was not some child to be reminded of such things. Her eggs suddenly lost all appeal. She pushed the plate away and stood up. "Then I suppose I should start getting ready now."

She heard her mother gasp but ignored the sound. Righteous anger carried her out of the room and up the stairs. But it dissipated as she considered the long hours before she could expect Mrs. Sheffield to arrive. She went back to the window and stared out at the rain.

❧

Although Alexandra had had plenty of time to get ready for the Sheffield's visit, she followed society's dictates and arrived downstairs "fashionably late." She entered the parlor, a smile of welcome on her face. At least the winter chill was being held at bay by the cheerful fire. Her gaze traveled around the room, coming to rest on the handsome countenance of Lowell Sheffield.

He stood when she entered and stepped forward as she dropped a curtsy. The warm kiss he pressed into the palm of her hand should have made her heart race, but it was cold and wet.

She shivered and pulled her hand free.

"How nice to see you, Miss Lewis."

"And you, Mr. Sheffield." She stepped past him to speak to his mother. "Welcome home, Mrs. Sheffield. I trust you had a pleasant Christmas."

The older lady inclined her head. "It was quiet."

"Too quiet." Lowell's voice tickled the curls at the nape of her neck. "I missed having our usual celebration."

"Yes, but there simply wasn't enough time to plan anything," said his mother.

Lowell put a hand under Alexandra's elbow and guided her toward a pair of chairs somewhat removed from the older ladies. "I have something to tell you."

All of Alexandra's doubt about his feelings disappeared. Lowell Sheffield was showing all the signs of a smitten suitor. "What is it?"

He shook his head. "You will have to come to a party my parents are hosting to find out."

"A party? Have you forgotten I am in mourning?"

"No, but I hope you can make an exception."

Mrs. Sheffield raised her voice slightly to include them in her conversation. "I was telling your grandmother of my plan to host a small party. Nothing large, just a few of the young people—"

"Will there be dancing?" Her grandmother did not wait for Mrs. Sheffield to complete her explanation. "You know she is still observing the proper mourning period."

"I will sit out any dances with your granddaughter," Lowell offered.

"And cause everyone to gossip about the two of you? I don't think that would be wise."

Disappointment hit Alexandra with the force of a blow, but she knew better than to argue with her strong-willed grandparent. "Perhaps you can come over the next day and tell me all about it."

Grand-mère made a tsking sound. "Did I say you could not go?" She turned to Mrs. Sheffield. "I don't know what to do with young people these days. They never listen."

"But I thought—"

A frown stopped her words. "I said Mr. Sheffield would start tongues wagging if he sat next to you for every dance. As long as I can rely on you to act circumspectly, I see no reason why you should not go."

"I'm glad you trust her to us." Mrs. Sheffield's smile was radiant. "I'll make sure she is taken care of."

Her grandmother nodded. "I know you will. When is this party taking place?"

"A week from today," Lowell answered for his mother. He leaned back against his chair, the picture of a wealthy young man in control of his destiny.

"Do you mean I have to wait a whole week to find out your surprise?" Alexandra gazed up at him and fluttered her eyelashes, a move that generally helped her get her way.

Lowell put a finger to his lips. "I have promised not to tell you yet."

Alexandra pouted at him but to no avail. He would not budge.

All too soon, his mother rose to her feet and gestured to him to join her.

"Until next week." He bowed over Alexandra's hand before escorting his mother from the parlor.

As they left, she could not help comparing Lowell Sheffield with the very different man who was residing at the Hugheses' home. Lowell would never be caught in public in his shirtsleeves. He was much too aware of his dignity. It was an attitude shared by most of the men she knew, an attitude she had always accepted as normal until she met Jeremiah LeGrand, a man who had no care for the cut of his clothing or the style of his hair.

Was that why Lowell Sheffield, who had once seemed so attractive, now appeared superficial and shallow to her?

eleven

"I still don't understand why you think I should attend this dinner." Jeremiah pulled on the cuff of his coat. It felt odd to wear formal clothing after so much time in the field.

"You have been working far too hard." Susannah's curls bounced as the carriage hit a rut. She turned to her husband. "Tell him, Judah."

"You've been working far too hard."

Jeremiah groaned and met his friend's gaze. "Traitor."

Judah spread his hands. "You should know by now you cannot win this argument."

A sigh from Susannah's corner of the carriage was long-suffering. "I don't know why I even try to help the two of you."

"Does that mean we can go back home?" Jeremiah raised his hand as if to knock on the wall separating his seat from the driver's bench.

"Don't you dare. We are going to this dinner. And you are going to enjoy yourself." Susannah's voice contained a note of exasperation. "I'll not have you telling your friends in New Orleans that we don't know anything about entertainment."

Jeremiah grunted. "I don't know when I've enjoyed myself more than the past months."

"I am glad to hear it." Judah shifted slightly. "But if you truly want to be a landowner, you should consider evenings like this one to be part of your duties. You never can tell who you will meet and what you will learn."

"It's not like this is my first dinner party."

"Excellent." Susannah patted his knee. "Then we won't have to worry about your ability to make civilized conversation."

"I have to talk, too? I thought all I had to do was eat."

Their laughter filled the carriage as they pulled up at

the Sheffields' home. Jeremiah exited the carriage first and offered his hand to Susannah. Then he waited patiently as Judah maneuvered his crutches. This was Judah's first party since coming back to Natchez. Jeremiah would have to watch out for his friend in the crowd.

Torches cast flickering light on the sidewalk leading to the graceful mansion. As they entered through the double doors, unobtrusive slaves took their wraps and disappeared. Jeremiah followed Susannah and Judah to the older couple who were waiting to welcome their guests. The Sheffields were typical hosts—well dressed, charming, wealthy. He exchanged greetings with them and walked into the parlor to meet the other guests.

These were the cream of Natchez society, the simpering debutantes and cosseted sons who would eventually lead the Mississippi territory into its future as a state. Lord, help them all. They made him feel old.

Susannah introduced him to several young women, but he forgot the previous girl's name as soon as the next one was brought forward. Some were prettier than others, some more graceful, but not one of them stirred the slightest bit of interest.

The room was beginning to grow crowded, and Jeremiah pulled at the starched collar that grew scratchier with each passing minute. Would they never sit down to their meal?

He glanced toward the door as another guest entered, her black dress in sharp contrast to all the other girls in the room. Alexandra.

She hesitated a moment, her dark eyes scanning the guests. When her gaze met his, something clicked in his mind, like a bolt being shot home. Or was something inside him being unbolted?

His mind went back to the first time he'd seen Alexandra. Her bravery had touched him then, and he had enjoyed being able to help her. But then he'd seen her in a different light, a more coquettish side of her which he found hard and unattractive. Which one was the real Alexandra?

He had to know the answer. He stepped forward, holding her gaze, trying to read the thoughts in her head. Those eyes of hers—soft as velvet and endless as the night sky—spoke to him. In them he read sadness and fear. She looked so lost for a moment, rousing his desire to rescue her once more.

Before he reached her side, it was gone. The connection between them was broken by the arrival of Lowell Sheffield at her side. Jeremiah watched as the other man, much more charming and urbane than he would ever be, bent over her hand and kissed it before tucking it into the crook of his elbow. He acted more like a suitor than a friend. His possessive attitude made Jeremiah's jaw clench, but he knew he couldn't pull her away from her escort without making a scene.

"So it really is Alexandra Lewis." A tall blond girl he was probably supposed to remember was standing next to him. "I couldn't believe it when Mrs. Sheffield said she would be attending tonight, but there she is. As bold as Jezebel."

Before he could decide whether or not to ask her what she meant, dinner was announced and another young man elbowed himself between them. "Miss Montgomery, I would be honored if you would allow me to escort you to the dining room."

Jeremiah bowed and left the two of them, going in search of the couple who had brought him here. He was going to wring a promise from Susannah never again to accept an invitation on his behalf. He would much rather spend the evening at home with a good book. Or even a bad one. Either way, the "conversation" would be more intelligent than what he was experiencing now.

❧

As much as she had looked forward to this evening, all Alexandra could think of was escape. She smiled at Lowell and allowed him to monopolize her attention. Obtaining his offer of marriage was her goal, after all.

She glanced at him and wondered again why he no longer

seemed appealing. He was handsome, rich, and kind, three things she valued most highly.

Lowell caught her staring and tilted his head toward hers. "What has put that frown between your eyes? Is something wrong with your food?"

"What?" She looked down at the untouched plate. "Oh no, of course not. The food is delicious." To prove the point she picked up her fork and speared a long bean, raising it to her mouth and nibbling at it in spite of the unsettled feeling in her stomach.

"Then it must be my presence that has put that sour look on your face."

"I apologize for my manners, Mr. Sheffield."

"Lowell, remember?"

"I apologize, Lowell. You must think my parents raised a very ungrateful child." She put down her fork and reached for her goblet. She lifted the crystal to her mouth and cool water rushed down her throat. She hoped it would settle her stomach, a stomach that had been churning since she realized that Dorcas Montgomery of Nashville was attending the party. Dorcas was the surprise Lowell had promised her.

A scornful smile turned up the corners of her lips. Some surprise. A friend from Nashville and one who knew the truth about her father's death. Would Dorcas share her knowledge with the Sheffields? She glanced down the table at the willowy blond. At least Dorcas was not one of the ones who had shunned her and her mother. Maybe her secret was safe.

"Not at all." He took the goblet of water from her hand and returned it to the table. "I think you are worried about something. Please trust me enough to tell me what is wrong."

"It's nothing." She grasped for an excuse that would satisfy him. "I'm a little worried about my mother. She is so sad in the evenings since Papa. . .died."

Lowell took her hand in his and raised it to his lips. "Your concern does you credit. You have a woman's tender heart."

Shame washed through her at his words. If only he knew how deceitful she really was. She had thought of her mother some this evening, but much more of her attention had gone to the girl sitting a few chairs down from them. "How do you know Dorcas?"

"My father and her father have done business in the past." He nodded toward Dorcas. "You probably know her family grows tobacco, and I'm sure you've heard how prices have fallen since the end of the war. Mr. Montgomery is thinking of trying to switch over to cotton. He wanted to purchase some of our seed and get my father's opinion on his chances of success. When we got ready to return, Ma asked Dorcas to come with us."

"I see."

"I've known Dorcas for years." He winked at her. "At one time, my parents and her parents thought we ought to make a match of it. But my taste doesn't run to blonds."

Normally, Alexandra would have dredged up some witty response to his comment, but her heart wasn't in it any longer. What had happened to her in the past weeks? She glanced away from Lowell and straight into the blue eyes that had haunted her dreams far too often. But in her dreams, the eyes were kind and caring. The gaze that skewered her now, however, was full of loathing. It took her back to her final weeks in Nashville and the hard-hearted people who had condemned her. Alexandra wanted to jump up from the table and run away, but she could not move.

Lowell had turned from her to answer a question from the person sitting on his other side.

Someone removed her plate and replaced it with a bowl of berries topped with fresh cream. She wondered where Mrs. Sheffield had procured fresh fruit at this time of year. It was surely an extravagance in the middle of winter.

Lowell had turned his attention to his dessert and wolfed it down in a few large bites before turning his attention back to her. "Are you ready to move to the ballroom?"

She put her spoon back on the pristine tablecloth, her dessert untouched. "Yes." Pushing back her chair and resting her hand on Lowell's arm, she lifted her chin and walked out of the room with all of the grace she could muster. The evening could not end soon enough for her.

The orchestra launched into their first piece as she and Lowell entered the ballroom. The polished floor would soon be scuffed by the movements of the eager dancers, but for now, it gleamed in the candlelight. Alexandra longed to throw off convention and let Lowell sweep her across the room in his arms.

Instead, she was engulfed in perfume as someone came up behind her and put her hands over Alexandra's eyes. "I bet you can't guess who this is."

Dorcas's accent, with its mountain twang, gave her away.

"It can be none other than the guest of honor." Alexandra pulled on the hands and turned around to see the golden-haired girl smiling at her oddly.

Dorcas giggled and hugged her. "Aren't you sweet? I've been waiting all night to get to say hello."

"It's nice to see you, Dorcas. How are you enjoying your stay in Natchez?"

"The Sheffields have been so considerate of my comfort that I feel like one of the family." She glanced toward Lowell, who was smiling at both of them. "But I have such good news for you, Alexandra."

Something in the tone of the other woman's voice put her on alert. She studied Dorcas's face, forcibly reminded of the content expression of a well-fed house cat. The room was filling up now as the rest of the dinner guests caught up with them. "Is that right?"

"Yes." Dorcas clasped her hands together and spoke a little louder. "The scandal about your father's death is dying down now. Hardly anyone is talking about the way he murdered that poor, innocent family. And the sheriff has fully recovered from the gunshot wound. I imagine you could even come back to Nashville and be received again."

Silence fell in the room. Heads turned toward them.

"Whatever are you talking about, Dorcas?" Lowell sounded as shocked as Alexandra felt.

"Oh no." Dorcas's eyes widened convincingly, but her smug grin told the true story. "Don't tell me I've spoken out of turn. I just assumed everyone knew. . . ."

"Knew what?" Now Lowell sounded exasperated.

"Please don't be angry with me, Lowell." She turned her gaze away from him, and Alexandra saw her eyes were moist. "How was I to know?"

Alexandra might have fallen for the ruse if she had not used it herself from time to time to convince others of her own innocence. "Dorcas is referring to the manner in which my father died last year."

Lowell took a step away from her, leaving Alexandra standing all alone in the crowded room. No one else was talking; even the orchestra had stopped playing as the musicians realized some drama was being played out.

"My father died under a cloud of suspicion." She glared at Dorcas, daring her to say anything more. "He was apparently involved in a plot to seize some valuable farm land from a family in the area."

"But I thought he was killed in an Indian raid?" Lowell's voice had hardened. He would probably blame her just like all those self-righteous people in Nashville.

"You are mistaken, Lowell." Alexandra took a deep breath. The words boiled around in her head, words that would condemn her to a life of shame. Her mouth was wobbly, making it hard for her to form the words properly, but she refused to let these people intimidate her. She clenched her jaw and forced the syllables out, one by one. "My father was killed in a shootout with the sheriff. Had he lived, he would most likely have been hung for his crimes."

A girl behind her gasped. Someone farther away asked what she had said. The buzz began slowly but gained momentum as her words were repeated to those who had not been able to hear for themselves.

Alexandra ignored all of them, even Dorcas, her attention centered on Lowell. Would he condemn her, too? Would he slip away from her as Asher had done? Was she doomed to lose each candidate she deemed suitable?

She saw the answer in his eyes and closed her own to hide the pain. She should have known better. She had been through this before. No one cared that she was innocent of the crimes her father had committed. She was guilty because she was his daughter. And the ironic thing about it was that she understood. She was one of these people. In the past, she would have separated herself from anyone with the barest hint of scandal, earned or not.

Alexandra pushed her way past Lowell and ran into the hallway. Tears swam in her eyes and overflowed onto her cheeks. Unable to see clearly, she barreled into someone. "Ex—excuse me."

"Alexandra. . .Miss Lewis. . .whatever is wrong?" The concerned voice made the tears flow harder.

"I. . .I have to g—get out of h—here."

A strong arm wrapped around her.

Alexandra burrowed into the reassuring warmth of a muscular chest. She was beyond caring who was holding her. All she knew was that her world had ended. . .again.

twelve

Jeremiah sent one of the hovering slaves to ready the Hugheses' carriage. "Don't worry. I'll see you safely home."

He frowned a warning at any of the guests who approached them. He had no idea what calamity had occurred before his arrival in the ballroom, but it didn't matter. What mattered was the crushed girl who was clinging to him like a half-drowned kitten. He stroked her back and murmured soft words of understanding and encouragement. He had no idea where the words came from, only that they were what she needed to hear right now.

Harvey Sheffield approached them warily. "The carriage is ready. Do you want me to get one of the slaves to accompany her?"

"I'll do it." Jeremiah wasn't going to let her be hurt anymore tonight. He was tempted to pick her up as he had that first night but decided to see if she could walk with his support. He helped her stand up and, keeping an arm around her, guided her to the front door.

It took a minute to sort out their wraps, but once they were both bundled up, he helped her into the carriage and took the seat opposite her, his back to the coachman. She seemed calmer now, only sniffling from time to time. Without comment, he gave her his handkerchief.

"Thank you."

"You're welcome."

She pushed herself into the far corner of the carriage. "Why are you being so nice to me?"

Jeremiah had been asking himself the same question. He didn't even know what she had done or what had been done to her. But he needed to get her mind off her troubles.

"A tent meeting has been going on across the river at Lake Concordia. I went to hear the preacher on Sunday. Do you know what book of the Bible he preached on?"

"No. How would I know?"

His eyes were growing accustomed to the darkness in the carriage. He could see her face now even though he could not make out her features. He imagined her brows were drawn together in a frown. "He spoke on John's first letter to his fellow Christians, specifically on John's instruction to love each other. 'Whosoever doeth not righteousness is not of God, neither he that loveth not his brother.' That verse really struck me. Our attempts to be honest and righteous are no more important than the love we show to each other."

The silence went on so long after he stopped speaking that Jeremiah wondered if she had fallen asleep. But then her husky voice answered him. "So you're seeing me home because it's your Christian duty?"

"I am ministering to a sister in Christ. I'm doing what I can to help someone God loves."

"I don't feel very lovable."

The heartrending catch in her voice made Jeremiah's eyes sting. "But you are so precious to God. Don't ever doubt it. He created you. He knew you even before you were born, and He loved you so much that He let His Son die on the cross for you."

Another silence.

"If that's true, then why did God let my father commit those terrible deeds? Why didn't He stop it from happening? Why didn't He protect me and my mother from the consequences of Papa's indiscretion?"

Jeremiah prayed for an answer that would heal the hurt in her heart. "People aren't reliable, Alexandra. Only God is. If you put your faith in another human being, you will always be disappointed. But if you turn to God, He will comfort you no matter what happens."

He could feel her gaze on him, but she didn't comment.

When the carriage pulled up at her family home, she stopped him from rising with a shake of her head. "I appreciate your kindness, but you should go back to the Sheffields'. Your friends will be worried about you."

Jeremiah nodded. He reached for her hand, squeezing it gently. "I'll be praying for you, Alexandra."

The party was ending by the time he returned, but Jeremiah heard all about what had happened from his friends on the ride home. It was a shame about Alexandra's father. A part of him could understand why her family had made up the story about Mr. Lewis dying a hero's death. But they must have known the truth would come out eventually. Now Alexandra and her mother would be forced to deal with the consequences. For their sakes, he hoped the scandal would blow over quickly. But if it didn't, at least they had family here who would stand by them.

Judah took a more conservative view of the evening's events. "I don't think it's a good idea for you to accept Alexandra any longer, Susannah."

The darkness of the carriage seemed to close in on Jeremiah. "You can't mean that."

"I have to protect my family's reputation."

"And what about your Christian duty to love others?"

"Jeremiah"—he could make out Susannah's blond curls as she leaned forward and shook her head—"don't be so hard on my husband. He's just a little confused. But don't worry. I'm not going to ostracize your Alexandra."

What was this? Had Susannah misunderstood his concern? "She's not my Alexandra. She's just a young woman who deserves our sympathy."

"Of course she is." Susannah's voice sounded a little choked, making him wonder if she was laughing at him. "And she shall get it. I promise you that."

thirteen

A shaft of sunlight woke Alexandra the next morning. No one had come in to light the fireplace in her room yet, so it must still be early. She burrowed deeper into the covers and tried to go back to sleep, but her mind wouldn't stop replaying the previous night's debacle.

She kept seeing Dorcas's face. She had known exactly what she was doing. But why? Did she harbor some grudge against Alexandra? She remembered the day they buried Papa and the feeling she'd had that Dorcas was looking for a reason to spread gossip about her. Perhaps it was simply her nature.

She pulled her knees up toward her chin. Gossip had always been a part of her world. She could remember the thrill of learning about one of her acquaintances in Nashville who had been caught embracing a man who was not her fiancé. It had been the talk at all the parties for several weeks. The whispers had grown to head shakes, and soon everyone was turning away from the indiscreet girl and her family.

Eventually the young man had asked to be released from the betrothal. At the time, Alexandra had joined the rest of her peers in condemning the girl's behavior. She deserved the treatment she had received. Didn't the Bible say people reaped what they had sown? The whole town had been in agreement. They had been united in their condemnation. No member of the family was exempted. Even the younger daughters were looked upon with suspicion.

At the time, it had never occurred to Alexandra to consider another interpretation of the events. She had never considered the pain they might be experiencing. Pain similar to what she felt this morning. But she had been innocent. She didn't deserve the treatment she would surely receive now that the truth was known.

Someone, probably Jemma, entered the room. She listened to the scrape of the iron poker stirring the warm coals, followed by the rhythmic *whoosh* of the bellows and the soft crackle of the fire. With a sigh she flipped back the counterpane.

"Good morning, Miss Alexandra." Jemma moved around the room, opening the curtains to allow more light to enter. "It's a pretty day."

"Not to me." Breakfast loomed in her mind like a towering thundercloud. She would have to tell her relatives that the scandal had caught up with them. "I wish I could sleep until noon."

Jemma's brown eyes widened. "Whatever is the matter?"

Alexandra supposed she might as well start practicing her story now. She swung her legs over the edge of the bed, her toes searching for her slippers. "An acquaintance of ours from Nashville was at the party last night. In fact, she was the reason for the party. And she kindly suggested that I could soon return to Nashville since Papa's scandal was no longer being discussed."

"Here you go." Jemma picked up her slipper and helped Alexandra ease her foot into it. "I suppose that's why you was crying last night."

A sigh of remorse filled her. Lowell would never want to marry her now. "What am I going to do?"

"Don't you worry none, miss. Things'll be all right."

"No they won't. No one will receive me anymore. It will be exactly like Nashville. The invitations will stop, and no one will come to visit. I'll never catch a husband like Grand-mère wants."

"Don't you be talking like that." Jemma pulled Alexandra's nightgown over her head and replaced it with a black cotton chemise. "You got so many blessings. Maybe this is God's way of getting you to share them."

Alexandra picked up her corset and stepped into it, tugging

upward until the stays enfolded her rib cage. She held it still while Jemma laced up the back. "What do you mean?"

The next layer of clothing was a dark petticoat, followed by a black overdress with long sleeves to protect her arms from the cold temperatures.

"There's lots of folks in Natchez who need help." Jemma shrugged and led her to the dressing table so she could fix Alexandra's hair. "Maybe God is freeing up your time so you can visit with them."

Preposterous. Spend her time helping the poor? Accompanying her aunt Patricia on more depressing visits? Yet what was the alternative? She could not stand the idea of sitting in the parlor, waiting for visitors who never arrived. Jeremiah's words from the evening before came back to her. He had shown her such kindness, coming to her rescue without question or concern for his own dignity. She opened her eyes and met Jemma's gaze in the mirror. "Maybe you're right."

Jemma beamed. "Once you show those people who you really are, they'll forget all about the past. You wait and see. They'll be knocking on your grandma's front door in no time. Nobody can resist a young lady with an open heart."

Alexandra left her and joined her family for breakfast. The gloom that had seemed so impenetrable earlier lifted a little. Once they saw the new Alexandra Lewis, her friends would be ashamed of their actions. And if they weren't, well, that was all right, too. She had no need of false friends. Like Jeremiah had told her last night, depending on human beings always brought disappointment. She was done with relying on others. She could count only on herself.

A thought struck her, and she turned on the staircase to look back at her bedroom door. Had God used Jemma to make her feel better this morning? Did He really care enough to involve Himself in her life? A spark of excitement warmed her, but then it faded. How ridiculous to think such foolishness. If He cared that much, why hadn't He been there when she really needed His help? Why had He been so silent during those days and weeks right after Papa's death? And why hadn't He stopped Papa from going down the wrong path?

No, believing in a caring, loving God was for children and old people. They needed to believe someone would protect them, be there for them. But she was young and healthy. She could make her own way in the world. She didn't need God or anyone else.

Neither Aunt Patricia nor Uncle John was present for breakfast. Alexandra had been so caught up in her own worries she had forgotten they were visiting his relatives and would be gone all day. Her plans to devote her time helping her aunt minister to the needy were dashed. What would she do with her day?

Grand-mère entered the dining room, leaning heavily on her cane. After she was seated and served, she turned to Alexandra. "How was your party last night?"

"It did not go as well as I had hoped."

Her mother, sitting across from her, looked up. "What happened?"

Alexandra wrung her napkin as if she could squeeze composure from it. "Do you remember the Montgomerys from Nashville?"

A wrinkle appeared in her mother's forehead.

"Well, no matter." Alexandra took a deep breath. "It seems Mr. Montgomery and Lowell's father have done business together for years. They went to Nashville—"

"Oh no." Mama's hand went to her mouth.

Alexandra nodded. "They brought Dorcas Montgomery back with them for a visit, and she announced to all the guests that Papa had been involved in a scandal. She was quite ingenuous, telling me we can most likely move back to Nashville now that all the talk has died down."

Her grandmother grunted. "At least no one knows the particulars."

"I'm fairly certain Dorcas gave them every scintillating detail once I left."

"Then you should have stayed and faced all of them down." Her grandmother pointed a gnarled finger toward her. "That's what's wrong with this world today. None of you young people have any gumption. Back when I was a young girl, I would have stood up to the lot of them. Made sure no one talked about me behind my back. If you'd have squared your shoulders and looked down your nose at this Dorcas, it would have all blown over by now."

"You weren't there, Grand-mère. Everyone was so shocked. Even Lowell couldn't look at me."

Her mother made a soft sound of sympathy.

The sharp knock of her grandmother's cane on the pine floor made Alexandra jump. "That young man will not go against the wishes of his family. And they know well enough that a marriage to the Tanner family will be advantageous. I have more than three times the acreage Harvey Sheffield can lay claim to."

Alexandra twisted her napkin in the other direction. "It's not always about money, Grand-mère. The Sheffields must look to their reputation."

Her grandmother looked toward her daughter. "Didn't you teach this girl anything, Beatrice?" She glared at Alexandra. "It's always, always, always about money. Money can polish any reputation, fulfill every dream, and buy every item your heart desires. As long as the Sheffields think they will benefit financially from a marriage with my family, they will make certain Lowell does not waver in his pursuit."

No sooner had her grandmother concluded her diatribe than the dining-room door opened, and one of the slaves entered. "You have visitors, Mrs. Tanner. Are you able to receive them?"

Her grandmother nodded. "Show them to the front parlor." The slave retreated to do her bidding, and Grand-mère returned her attention to Alexandra. "Now do you believe me?"

Alexandra pushed her chair back from the table. She felt a little sick. All this time she'd thought Lowell was interested in her. To find that he was only interested in her family's money was quite a blow to her ego. Only an hour earlier, she would have rejoiced in his appearance at her home. Now she only wanted to retreat to her bedroom and hide from the world.

fourteen

"It's really too early to be making a morning call." Jeremiah shook his head at Susannah. "I tried to warn you that we would be kept waiting until the Tanners break their fast."

"I only wanted to make sure none of them was upset about last night. Miss Lewis seemed so distraught."

Jeremiah glanced toward her husband and shook his head.

"I don't care what you say. I know you care about her, too." Susannah's glance was smug.

Judah moved his crutches to one side and put his free hand on Jeremiah's shoulder. "How many times is it that you've rescued Miss Lewis?"

"Actually it was your carriage that rescued her the first time." Jeremiah twisted his lips into a slight smile. "Come to think of it, your carriage was the rescuer last night, too."

Susannah laughed. "And I suppose you had absolutely nothing to do with it?"

"I'm not saying that. I was there at the right time to lend a hand. God has been kind enough to use me to aid a Christian sister in need."

The door opened and the ladies of the Tanner household entered. Mrs. Tanner led the way, leaning heavily on her cane, followed by Alexandra's mother and then Alexandra herself. Her face seemed so pale, and smudges under her eyes bespoke a restless night. His heart went out to her. She seemed so fragile, nothing like the aristocratic belle who had treated him as if he was inconsequential when she first saw him. Even though he would not have wished this pain on her, perhaps God would use it to mold her into a woman who cared about the needs of those outside her immediate family.

Once they had all exchanged greetings, Mrs. Tanner told them all where to sit. Judah and Susannah were relegated to a pair of delicate chairs while he was told to take a seat on the far side of the fireplace, opposite the sofa on which Alexandra and her mother sat.

Mrs. Tanner took up her seat, an oversized chair with cushions that made him think of a throne. "To what do we owe this pleasure?" The older lady went straight to the point.

Susannah leaned forward and caught Alexandra's gaze. "We just wanted to check on you after the party and make certain you know you have friends here."

Mrs. Tanner stamped her cane on the floor. "Of course the girl has friends. She's an accomplished young lady with an outstanding pedigree. She's the most eligible female in Adams County, maybe in the Mississippi Territory."

Jeremiah hid a smile. It was fitting for her to defend Alexandra. She reminded him of Uncle Emile. He'd never allow any slur against his nephew.

A glance at Alexandra showed her discomfort with the direction of the conversation. Time to introduce a new subject. "What do you think of the talk of statehood?"

Alexandra's mother looked out the window, obviously unwilling to join the discussion. Or maybe she had no opinion on the matter of politics.

Mrs. Tanner, however, did not share her daughter's diffidence. "I think it's a load of hogwash."

"What about the protection of the army?" Susannah folded her hands in her lap. "And so many immigrants are arriving now that the war is over. We need law and order or we risk falling into chaos."

Judah nodded, smiling at his wife. "I agree. One thing the politicians in Washington should have learned is how important this part of our continent is. If the British had taken New Orleans, no treaty would have stopped their advance up the river. Every settlement, including Natchez, would have been raided. The men would have been impressed into the British services and the crops would have been seized to support the invaders."

"So they should know enough to protect us whether we remain a state or a territory." Mrs. Tanner's smug gaze traveled the room.

"But wouldn't you like to have some say in who is running the territory?" Alexandra entered the conversation. "You always say President Madison should not have the power to decide who will govern us. If we become a state, we will have the right to elect our leaders."

Jeremiah was impressed with Alexandra's comments. She might be pampered, but she was not empty-headed. "Do you think the territory should be made into one state or two?"

A frown appeared in her brow as Alexandra considered his question. "Since the Indian lands were included in the territory, it has become a huge square, much larger than any of the other states."

"But we don't have many people living in that area, especially on the eastern side of the territory."

"As Susannah said, immigrants seem to be pouring into the territory in ever-growing numbers. Who knows where it will end?" Alexandra shrugged. "Of course I could be wrong. I have never traveled to the eastern portion of the territory. Perhaps it should be one state."

"Well, one advantage of making two states is the increased number of senators who would represent the area."

An arrested look entered her face. "I see. That makes a great deal of sense. So do you think there should be two states?"

"I don't think it much matters what any of us in this room thinks." Judah spoke before Jeremiah could answer. "We won't be involved in the decision-making process."

"Too true, dear." Susannah accepted a cup of tea from Alexandra. "And perhaps that is best."

Alexandra continued pouring cups of the strong brew and passing them out. Jeremiah took a tentative swallow of his drink. The dark liquid stung the inside of his mouth, but it wasn't too bitter for his taste.

"Are you still working in the cotton fields, Mr. LeGrand?" Alexandra's face looked more relaxed than it had when she first entered the parlor.

Susannah stirred a lump of sugar into her tea. "He's single-handedly brought things back from the edge of disaster. Thanks to his hard work, we'll be able to pay our taxes and buy seed for the spring planting."

Now it was Jeremiah's turn to squirm. He did not like to brag about what he'd been doing.

"Yes, I've heard about things over at Magnolia Plantation." Mrs. Tanner refused a cup of tea. "And not all of it is good."

"What do you mean?" asked Judah.

"My granddaughter told me about his penchant for working next to the slaves. It's not good to coddle them. It leads to dissatisfaction and perhaps even a slave revolt."

Jeremiah nodded. He could understand that his way of doing things might seem odd, even threatening to the other landowners. A large number of black slaves lived in the territory. Most whites believed the only way to maintain control was to keep their slaves too exhausted and too detached to foment rebellion. He disagreed. To him it made more sense to give the slaves land of their own to work and chances to earn their freedom if they wished to do so. He had a lot of plans that would not meet with the approbation of people like Mrs. Tanner. He wished he could openly discuss his ideas. Maybe one day. But for now, he should concentrate on the young lady they'd come to see. "I'm sure you have more experience than I do, Mrs. Tanner."

"Jeremiah is very humble." Susannah's voice held a note of censure. Jeremiah wondered if it was aimed at him or at Mrs. Tanner. "He is a successful businessman in his own right. Did you know he and his uncle have one of the most successful shipping businesses in New Orleans? And he has postponed his plans because of his insistence on helping us get back on our feet."

Jeremiah frowned at Susannah. He didn't need anyone to defend him. "I believe in helping others when I can. God has blessed me greatly so that I can pass blessings on to others in His name."

"That's easy for you to say." The anger in Alexandra's voice was hard to miss. "What do you know about losing a parent?"

Judah's mouth dropped open, and silence invaded the room.

Jeremiah folded his arms across his chest. "You're quite right, Miss Lewis. I don't remember my parents at all. You see, they died when I was a child."

The look on her face, a combination of horror, shame, and sympathy, was something he would never forget. It was hard to suppress the smile trying to curl his lips. A laugh fought its way up his throat, but Jeremiah pushed it back down.

"I'm so sorry." She was the picture of remorse, her hands folded in her lap, her eyes trained on the tips of her feet.

Jeremiah was ashamed of himself. He should have let her words stand. Why had he felt it necessary to embarrass her? He was usually much more circumspect. "You could not have known."

She glanced up at him, and he was surprised to see the sheen of tears in her eyes. "That doesn't excuse my tantrum. Please say you forgive me."

"Forgiven and forgotten." He smiled at her to show her his words were true.

"Good for you, young man. My granddaughter is a pretty thing, but she's easily provoked to anger—a trait her parents should have rid her of many years ago."

Jeremiah had turned to give his attention to Mrs. Tanner, but he saw Alexandra's chin lift from the corner of his vision.

"Please, Grand-mère." Her voice was strained.

He wished he'd never defended himself. When he'd agreed to come with his friends, it was with the hope of making her feel better, not to add to her discomfort.

He looked at Susannah, who nodded and put her cup on

the table at her elbow. "I am hoping to get you ladies to come to my house on Thursday for some of my special mint tea and a few hours of quilting."

Jeremiah had expected Susannah to announce their departure, not invite Alexandra and her family for a visit.

"I don't—"

Alexandra's refusal was overridden by her grandmother. "They would love to. Both my daughters and Alexandra accept your kind offer."

"Excellent." Susannah stood.

Judah and Jeremiah followed suit, bowing to the women and taking their leave as usual. As they gathered their wraps and headed out the door, Jeremiah could hear Mrs. Tanner telling Alexandra and her mother why they would be visiting the Hugheses' home on Thursday. He needed to make sure he was not at the house at that time. Maybe he and Judah could look for a place to house Uncle Emile's new office. It was about time for him to concentrate on his other reason for coming to Natchez.

He nodded to himself. It was the perfect excuse for avoiding further contact with Alexandra.

fifteen

It was raining when Jeremiah awoke on Thursday morning. He groaned and dressed with more care than usual. His excuse for not being available when the visitors arrived had disappeared when the weather turned inclement. He couldn't even go out and work with the slaves. Or could he? As he headed downstairs, plans began to evolve in his head. He would need to time things right if he was going to avoid Miss Alexandra Lewis. And avoiding her was of paramount importance to him.

Breakfast was a hurried affair. He ignored Susannah's pointed comments and headed outside. The rain beat steadily on the barn's roof as Jeremiah checked the tack for wear.

Noise outside indicated when she arrived. Jeremiah's heart beat a rapid tattoo in response. What was Alexandra wearing today? Would her hair be pulled back in a tight bun? Or would it be styled in ringlets to frame her face? He shook his head to clear it. Why did it matter?

The easy answer was that it shouldn't matter to him at all. But Jeremiah was not in the habit of accepting easy answers. The subject would take some serious soul searching. Nothing about Alexandra should affect him beyond the consideration he would offer to any sister in Christ. But the rat-a-tat of his heart told a different story. What was it about her that made him feel so. . .so agitated? Jeremiah knew he could not be falling in love with her.

His mind rejected the idea before it was fully formed. In the first place, he did not know Alexandra. He'd only been around her a few times, and their conversation had been limited. She *was* more than the shallow debutante he'd first thought her to be. She was beautiful and smart, but that didn't mean she was the woman God intended for his mate.

Which brought up the most important reason he could *not* have feelings for Alexandra: She depended on others for happiness and acceptance, not on the Lord. She might be the sweetest, most unassuming young woman in the territory, but if she didn't love the Lord with all her heart, she was not a woman he could share—

The sound of the barn doors opening and closing brought him out of the tack room. There she stood, dressed in black, her hair loosely pulled back and pinned at the nape of her neck. Her hands were folded in front of her, and she was looking around the shadowy barn with all the innocence of a baby bird.

"What do you want, Miss Lewis?"

She jumped at the sound of his voice and put one hand up to her throat. "Oh, you gave me a fright, Mr. LeGrand. Susannah sent me to remind you that tea will be served in a few minutes."

He could feel heat rising to his cheeks. Susannah shouldn't be playing the matchmaker. How aggravating. He would have to talk with her later. But for now, he needed to rid himself of the beauteous Miss Lewis. "I won't be taking tea with you today. I have too much work to do."

She walked to where he stood outside the tack room. The fresh scent of her lemony perfume seemed to flow over him like warm bathwater. "Why do you dislike me so much? Have you not forgiven me for mistaking you for a servant? I am very sorry for offending you."

"What?" He looked down at her in surprise. "What makes you think I dislike you?"

She shrugged and twisted her hands together. "You seem to make it a point to avoid me whenever I come to visit."

"I have a great deal of responsibility these days and very little time for social visits." He tugged at the collar of his shirt, which had suddenly grown uncomfortably snug. He knew he was not being completely truthful with her, but how could he be? How could he admit he was no stronger than any of the other men who chased after her? That some part of him wanted to protect her from all danger? How could he tell her that his heart was pounding even now because he wanted to reach out and touch her soft hair?

"I see." She glanced up at him, a wounded look in her eyes. "I suppose I should go back inside."

"I suppose so." He didn't move, and neither did she. He felt like an idiot, but he couldn't think of a thing to say to her. All he wanted to do was stare into those dark brown eyes.

After what seemed an eternity, though it couldn't have been more than a minute or two, she sighed and turned away. "It was nice to see you again."

He didn't answer. His throat worked, but he couldn't get any words to come out. He watched as she moved away from him and wished he could say something to stop her. But what was the point? He'd already gone over this. He didn't—couldn't—care for Alexandra Lewis.

sixteen

Aunt Patricia was delighted when Alexandra asked to accompany her as she made her rounds. The first place they stopped was a small shack just north of the plantation grounds.

"Who lives here?" Alexandra avoided a clucking chicken as she helped carry several baskets of warm food toward the shack.

"An old black man, Tobias Jenkins. His master died a few years back, and he and the other slaves were set free by the widow. John wanted to give him some land, but your grand-mère refused. So John and I bought a little parcel off the plantation grounds and gave it to him. He started off fine but caught the croup last winter. Since then, it's been difficult for him to keep body and soul together."

"Doesn't he have any family or friends to help him?"

Aunt Patricia shook her head. "He had a wife, a woman he jumped the broom with, but she died shortly after they were freed. There's no one else." She slid the wicker handle of her basket toward her elbow and reached out with the other hand to knock on the door.

"Who's there?"

Alexandra could hear hacking coughs coming from the little house.

"It's Mrs. Patricia and my niece Alexandra. We've come with some stew for you and medication to ease that cough."

The door swung open slowly, creaking on its hinges. A small man with the darkest face Alexandra had ever seen looked out at them.

Aunt Patricia performed quick introductions, and they went inside, placing their baskets on the hearth in front of a roaring fire.

The interior of the small home was much cozier than the exterior indicated. A quilt covered the mattress of a narrow bed, its bright colors giving a cheerful feel to the room. A rocking chair stood next to the fireplace, obviously the seat the old man used. A small table was nestled in the corner of the large open space, two chairs pulled up to it.

Tobias pointed to the chairs. "Why don't you turn those around and have a seat next to the fire." He moved slowly toward the table and held up a knife over a loaf of dark bread. "Would you care for a slice? I made this two days ago."

Aunt Patricia shook her head as she settled into one of the chairs. "We ate before we came, Tobias."

He began coughing as he put the knife back on the table.

The hacking sounded awful to Alexandra's ears. She stood and helped the man walk across the room and sit down in his rocker. "Can I fetch some water for you?"

Tobias shook his head. It took a few moments, but he finally got the coughing back under control. "You're a kind young lady." His face had lost some of its color, taking on the hue of river mud. "It seems to come natural in your family."

His words stung her conscience like tiny barbs. "I haven't been very much interested in helping until now."

"It doesn't matter when you start." Aunt Patricia smiled at her. "Only that you do." She turned to Tobias. "How have you been doing?"

He shrugged, wiping his mouth with a white handkerchief. "Not too bad."

"I worry about whether or not you're eating regularly."

"It doesn't take much to feed a lazy old man." He grinned at them, showing both of the teeth he had. "Now come spring, when I get to planting my garden, it may take something more to keep up my energy, but I've saved a little money. I'll be able to barter with the merchants in Natchez to buy what I need."

Aunt Patricia rolled her eyes. "Don't try to fool me. You haven't been able to work since last winter. I doubt you have more than fifty cents to your name."

Alexandra watched as her aunt, the daughter of a wealthy landowner, bantered with the friendly man. The woman she'd thought of as starchy and uninteresting was showing a completely different side of herself. She was smiling and laughing and looked a decade younger than she had as they rode over to the cabin. It was as though she was gaining as much from this visit as Tobias was.

"I suppose we had best get on our way, Alexandra." Aunt Patricia stood and picked up the cloak she had laid across the back of her chair. "We have several stops to make before dinner."

Even though the cold air nipped at her nose as Alexandra followed her aunt back out to the carriage, contentment warmed her through and through. Maybe she would actually enjoy dispensing goods to the needy.

After several similar stops, her aunt instructed the coachman to take them home. "We need to get back. A lot of work is waiting for us there."

Alexandra settled into a corner of the coach opposite her aunt. "What kind of things do you have in mind?"

"Your uncle and I were down at Natchez Under-the-Hill last week, and we saw many poor, tired immigrants passing through on their way to who knows where. You should have seen them. Exhausted and scared, ragged and hungry. The children were so thin their little arms looked like knobby sticks, and their parents were not in much better shape. They need everything from warm meals to cloaks and blankets. Most of them sold all their belongings just to get to America."

Her memory dredged up a dreary picture of the waterfront, and Alexandra's heart melted. "What a wonderful idea. It sounds as if they need our help."

"Yes, they do. I found a whole stack of blankets we no longer use because they have holes in them. So we are going to mend them and take them to the waterfront for those poor souls."

Anticipation made her toes curl. Alexandra could hardly wait to get started. "I hope you know you have changed my outlook. I mean. . ." She paused, searching for the right words to express her thoughts.

Aunt Patricia reached across the carriage and patted her hand. "I know what you mean, dear. There's nothing like ministering to others to remind us of the many blessings we have."

seventeen

"I have an idea." Jeremiah's statement elicited a groan from his friend. He looked out of the carriage as it traveled the road to town. He and Judah had been planning this trip for several days. A piece of property was being offered for sale that should make an excellent shipping office, and Jeremiah wanted to purchase it if the building was in good shape and the price was fair.

"The last time you said that to me, we ended up spending the whole day across the river at that tent meeting."

"You have to admit the minister was a great speaker. The Spirit was using him to deliver a message we needed to hear."

Judah laughed. "He was good, but it's a wonder we didn't catch colds after all that time out in the open. Ferriday Plantation may not be that far away, but crossing the river at this time of year exposed us to some raw weather."

"I still think it was worth the trouble." Jeremiah remembered the hours spent hanging on every word the minister delivered. A part of him wished he had the talent to teach the Word, but he had not been gifted in that way. He was able to share the Gospel with people one-on-one and even sometimes in a group of five or so, but he was not an orator. "But back to my idea. What would you think of ordering slate tablets and pencils?"

"Whatever for? Who are you planning to teach?"

Jeremiah turned his attention away from the landscape. "I was thinking about showing your slaves the rudiments of reading and writing."

Judah crossed his arms over his chest and grunted. "You can forget your revolutionary ideas. I know things were different where you grew up, but here slaves are the labor force that makes our crops profitable. If we teach the slaves to read, they will clamor for freedom. How do you think things would go at home if I freed all the slaves?"

"I believe you could hire them to work for you instead of forcing them to do so. Can't you see enslavement is wrong? The men and women you 'own' are precious in the Lord's sight."

"They are precious to me, too. . .precious to the smooth operation of the plantation." Judah frowned at him. "You'd better keep your ideas to yourself. Many people in this county would lynch you for the ideas you've espoused to me."

"Do I need to fear a vicious mob attack?"

"No, but you may get a very chilly reception if you start ordering school supplies for slaves. It's not legal. If word got out, you would go to jail. The people around here don't take kindly to newcomers messing with the system that's been in use for decades."

Jeremiah considered the advice. His friend had grown up here and knew the people. But that didn't mean Jeremiah's plan was doomed to failure. It would simply be placed on a back shelf for now. As soon as he got the shipping business up and running, he could use his uncle's contacts. It shouldn't be a problem to have a few dozen tablets and pencils ordered.

"It's a nice day." Judah leaned forward to look out of the window. "Spring will be upon us soon."

"Indeed." As Jeremiah watched the passing scenery, his mind wandered back to the idea for a school. He could have a new building raised on the plantation grounds. That way, few of the planters would realize his plans until they were underway. It could be about the same size as the sewing house, unpretentious and simple, with several desks and a tablet for each person in attendance. He could start with the children who were too young to be put to work. Then they could go home every day and show their parents and older siblings what they had learned.

The coach passed a wide road leading west into a dense

forest. "Is that the drive to a plantation home?" Jeremiah asked.

Judah glanced past him and shook his head. "That's Liberty Road."

"Good name." He encouraged his friend to elaborate with a nod.

"Several hunting lodges down that road are owned by some of the most prosperous planters around here. They don't get down there very often, but they have slaves on duty all the time. As long as the masters are not in residence and the lodges are cared for, the slaves are free to do what they will with their time. They have much more liberty than you would expect."

"Why don't they run away?"

A shrug answered him. "I guess they are comfortable."

Jeremiah couldn't imagine living in a half-world of slavery. "Until the master comes. Then they have to give up their freedom again. It seems to me that would be a painful process."

"Not as painful as being whipped or branded if they are caught without papers. Since our neighbors up north have been threatening to shackle the Southland by outlawing slavery, things have gotten much more tense. Catching a runaway slave has always been serious business, but it's even more so since slaves who make it to certain states or territories in the North are considered free."

"I wonder where it will end."

"From what we've learned since returning to Natchez, the price of cotton is rising daily. Our economy strengthens with each shipment." Judah shifted his position on the cushioned bench. "The system works because our slaves work."

Jeremiah couldn't agree with Judah. "There must be a way to make plantations successful without the enslavement of human beings."

"Maybe so." Judah's expression had drawn into a frown. "I've never purchased a slave myself."

"But you've not considered freeing the ones you inherited."

"I'm not as wealthy as you, Jeremiah. If I freed the slaves,

Susannah and I would lose everything."

Jeremiah recognized the fear in his friend's voice. "It wouldn't be easy, but you and your wife should consider other ways to make the plantation profitable. Perhaps you could free a few at a time to make it easier on you."

"I'll think about it."

They arrived in town and found the property Jeremiah wished to inspect. It was a brick building clinging to the edge of the bluff overlooking Natchez Under-the-Hill. They went inside and found a pair of small rooms in the front of the building that could be used as office space and a set of rooms upstairs that could be updated for a living space.

"I can see a large desk in that room, and you with your feet up on it while you count all the money you earn." Judah's teasing words made Jeremiah laugh.

"I'm much more likely to be down at the waterfront making sure the shipments find their way to the correct boats."

"Once you get this place fixed up, I cannot imagine wanting to leave it. I can almost hear the deals being made between your business and the local farmers." Judah hobbled across the room and looked out a dirt-streaked window. "They'll be lining up outside to sell you their cotton."

Jeremiah watched his friend, glad to see the liveliness in his expression. It was good to see Judah animated. He seemed to have forgotten his infirmity for a few moments. If only Judah could stay here and run things. . . It would give Jeremiah more time to do what he wanted to do—work the land and make meaningful changes.

Inspiration struck as suddenly as a summer storm. "What would you think of managing the business for me?"

Judah turned so quickly he almost fell over. "I. . .I don't know the least thing about the shipping business."

"I can teach you what you'll need to know." Jeremiah's voice grew more certain as the details fell into place in his mind. "You can start by making inquiries in town for the furniture we'll need."

"That's ridiculous. I'm a farmer. If it wasn't for this leg. . ." He waved a hand downward as his voice faded.

Jeremiah dropped his chin and raised an eyebrow. "Instead of focusing on your problems, you should consider my suggestion. You would be a natural." Certainty flooded him. He knew this was right. All he had to do was convince his friend.

Judah's serious gaze wandered around the room. "I don't know. . . ."

Silence invaded the room as Jeremiah waited for his hesitant friend to think about his idea. A prayer filled his heart. Would this be the right path for Judah? And what about Susannah?

Judah turned back to him, excitement animating his face. "Hickman O'Grady made a couple of the pieces we have at home. He has a shop a few blocks away. We can go see what he might have to offer in the way of furnishings."

"I'll leave that up to you. I need to go by the bank and make a few other stops." Jeremiah withdrew his pocket watch. "I'll meet you back here in a couple of hours."

Judah nodded and made his way to the door.

Jeremiah could hear his friend's excited voice directing the coachman. He glanced toward the ceiling, the grateful outpouring of David's Psalm 103 filling his heart. " 'Bless the Lord, O my soul: and all that is within me, bless his holy name.' Thank You, Lord. You are so faithful to Judah and to me."

The future opened up in front of him, stunning him with its possibilities. God had blessed him beyond his greatest imaginings.

eighteen

Alexandra gazed at the dresses comprising her wardrobe. Should she choose the black silk with gray rosettes? Or the black bombazine with its gray fichu? Or maybe the black taffeta skirt unrelieved by any hint of color. She looked toward Jemma. "You pick one of them."

Jemma shook her head. "Now, Miss Alexandra, you're too partic'lar for that."

She raised her gaze to the ceiling and blew out a breath of disgust. "They're all black, so what does it matter?"

The way her slave stared at her made Alexandra's cheeks flush. She looked at the faded brown homespun dress Jemma always wore. She knew she ought to be grateful for what she had. Things could be worse—she and Mama could be homeless, working their fingers to the bone washing clothes or making soap. Then she wouldn't have to worry what to wear because, like Jemma, she would own only one dress.

She finally pointed to the dress with the nice fichu. "I want to look my best in church without overdoing it."

Jemma picked up the dress and helped her get it over her petticoat, tugging and fussing until each fold of material was hanging just so. Then she tweaked a few strands of hair that had been mussed. "Will you be wearing your hat, or did you want the lace scarf?"

Alexandra considered a moment before choosing the gray scarf and sitting down in front of her dressing table. Jemma fastened the delicate material over her hair with several pins. When it was secure, Alexandra rose and picked up her fan and the black reticule that would hold her handkerchief and a few hairpins. "I believe I am ready."

"Yes, ma'am. You look real nice."

"Thank you, Jemma." Alexandra went downstairs to meet the other members of her family.

"Put on your cloak so we can get started." Grand-mère rose slowly and looked her over with a discerning gaze. "And remember to hold your head high. The way to deal with burgeoning scandal is to face it head on."

Alexandra wanted to run back upstairs and refuse to come out, but she knew her grandmother would never allow such behavior. She didn't want to face anyone, not with the memory of Lowell's frozen features so clear in her mind. What if he cut her? She glanced at her grandmother and decided with a lift of her chin that she would never let them see her discomfiture.

"That's the spirit, girl." Her grandmother allowed a cloak to be settled across her bent shoulders. "Don't ever forget you're as good as any of them. Your grandfather and I settled in this area long before most of the upstarts we'll see this morning. You have nothing to hang your head about."

The carriage ride was bumpy. And crowded. Squeezed between Aunt Patricia's generous curves and her mother's angular bones, Alexandra wished she could have sat outside with the driver. At least then she could see the ruts ahead and brace herself. She was certain she would be black and blue before evening.

Their arrival caused a bit of a stir, probably because the service had already begun by the time they entered the church. Alexandra could feel the weight of curious gazes as they walked down the central aisle in search of available seats. She knew her grandmother had wanted them to arrive late as if in defiance of anyone's disapprobation.

The pastor halted in the middle of leading a congregational hymn. "Welcome, Mrs. Tanner. I'm glad you and your family could join us."

Grand-mère inclined her head before waving her hand. "You may continue, Preacher."

A wave of giggles swept the congregation. The pastor's

cheeks reddened. He cleared his throat, adjusted his spectacles, and resumed the hymn. When he had finished leading the congregation in singing, he began his sermon by reading the Sermon on the Mount from Matthew's gospel. " 'Blessed are they that mourn: for they shall be comforted.' "

Alexandra wanted to get up and walk out. Jesus' promises were empty. When Papa died, no one was there to comfort her or Mama. She reached for her mother's hand and squeezed. *Never mind,* she wanted to tell her mother. *I am here for you even if God is not.*

Her mother's hand was so cold. She seemed to be fading away right in front of her family. She went through the motions of living—needlework in the parlor, eating meals in the dining room, responding when she was asked a question. But Alexandra could not think of a single conversation her mother had initiated since their arrival in Natchez. She remembered how much she had hoped coming home would help her mother cope with the grief, but nothing seemed to pierce the fog that surrounded her.

How Alexandra wished she could make things better. Would marriage to Lowell make a difference? She looked around surreptitiously for his familiar features, and her gaze locked with Dorcas Montgomery's. She was reduced in an instant to the level of a child. She wanted to stick out her tongue at the woman or scrunch her face into an ugly expression. Instead, she smiled sweetly. The look on Dorcas's face turned as sour as old milk. Alexandra's smile widened. Keeping her composure had its benefits.

She turned her head in the other direction and wondered how she could have missed the fiery reddish-blond hair and broad shoulders of the man sitting at the far end of their pew. Jeremiah LeGrand was studying his Bible as if it held the answer to all of life's difficulties. She could feel her nostrils flaring. Did he really believe what the pastor was saying? Apparently so.

He was quite the conundrum to her. He'd been so kind on

the ride home in the carriage after the disaster at Lowell's home, yet he had not hesitated to reprimand her when she'd been rude. And then in the Hugheses' barn, for a moment she thought she saw attraction in his gaze. But when she'd tried to let him know she was receptive, he had retreated behind an impenetrable wall.

Her grandmother cleared her throat and shook her head at Alexandra. Chastened, the young woman returned her attention to the pulpit.

The pastor had apparently finished with the New Testament. "When Job heard he had lost all of his cattle and children, he mourned greatly, but he refused to turn from God. His wife told him he should, but Job held onto his faith, and even though he had to face many trials and doubts before God restored him, he was restored." He flipped through the pages of his Bible. "The Bible says he was blessed to receive even more than he had lost, including livestock, three beautiful daughters, and seven sons."

Alexandra wondered if God would return her to the prosperity, hope, and happiness she had once enjoyed. She didn't see how it was possible. Not after what had happened at Lowell's house. Neither he nor anyone else was going to want to marry her. She would probably end up an old maid living off Grand-mère's generosity. Or maybe there was some old widower who would marry her in spite of the scandal. She shuddered at the thought and hoped things would not get that desperate.

Perhaps Uncle John and Aunt Patricia would give her some land like they had done for Tobias. But then how would she manage? She couldn't imagine washing her own clothes, growing her own food, or even trying to keep her house clean. No, she needed to find a husband. Someone who would care for her and give her back the things she used to have.

"I think one of the lessons of Job is to trust God to have our best interests at heart. God sometimes allows us to be tested, but He is always there waiting for us to turn to Him. Once we do, He is faithful to deliver us."

Alexandra considered the man's words as he prayed to end the service. She followed her family out of the church, waving to Susannah and Judah. She was unable to get close enough to them to speak because of the crush of the people in the aisle.

Grand-mère took her time, making sure to stop and speak to anyone who was anyone.

Someone's elbow dug into her side, nearly oversetting Alexandra, and a large hand wrapped around her waist.

"Excuse me." She glanced up to see who had saved her from an embarrassing tumble. Jeremiah's face was only inches from her own, causing her heart to flutter. Her breath caught, and for an instant, it seemed they were the only ones in the room. He smiled at her, showing those intriguing dimples, and her lips trembled into a weak smile. But then reality intruded. What must this man think of her? That she was always in need of rescuing? She pulled away from him. "Let me go."

"Pardon me." His hand fell away. "I was worried you would fall."

Someone else jostled her, and Alexandra was pushed back against his broad chest with a soft *oof*. His hand captured her elbow, his arm warm across her back. Perhaps she did need someone to keep her safe. But why did his touch send her heart climbing up her throat?

Safe in the shelter of his strength, Alexandra allowed herself to be guided to the front door. She barely noticed when her grandmother stopped to speak to Governor Holmes, the affable man chosen by President Jefferson, when he was still in office, to govern the territory. Everyone said he would make a good governor if Mississippi ever gained statehood. She smiled and curtsied when Grand-mère introduced her. The governor bowed and turned to greet the man standing next to her. Her mind was too preoccupied with her reaction to Jeremiah's closeness to pay attention to the conversation.

Another voice, one that sounded petulant in contrast to Jeremiah's deep tones, called her name. Alexandra turned and felt her heart thump back into place. "Lowell, h–how are you doing?"

He looked as handsome as ever, and was that contrition she saw in his gaze? "I'm so glad to see you this morning. I've wanted to talk to you about what happened. . .you know, about what Dorcas said."

Now her traveling heart moved further downward, apparently reaching toward her toes. She realized Jeremiah had stopped talking. She could feel both men's gazes on her. Both listening intently. Alexandra licked her lips and raised her chin. "If you wanted to apologize for your boorish behavior in not defending my reputation, all you had to do was come to visit, something you've done any number of times since my arrival." How amazing that she had managed to get all those words out without the slightest stumble.

Dorcas came out of the church then and walked toward them.

Not wanting to hear anything that woman had to say, Alexandra turned away. . .and met Jeremiah's intense gaze. What was he thinking? Was he sympathetic to her dilemma? Or appalled at her outspokenness?

Her heart clenched at the possibility of his disapproval. Before he could confirm her worst fear, Alexandra hurried to her grandmother's carriage. She'd better have her relatives send for the doctor. Something was definitely wrong with her heart.

nineteen

Sunday luncheon was an interminable affair. Alexandra pushed her food around on her plate while her grandmother relived every moment of the church service, including Alexandra's tirade at Lowell Sheffield.

"You did very well, my dear." The gray-haired woman pointed a finger at Alexandra. "You administered quite the set down. I don't doubt that young man will come by before the day is over."

Alexandra could not dredge up any excitement over the idea of entertaining Lowell. Why did she wish it was Jeremiah who would be coming to visit instead of Lowell? "You may be right, Grand-mère. But it's amazing how little I care."

Mama looked up at her rebellious tone. "Alexandra, whatever is wrong with you? You know what you must do."

Now her mother wanted to rejoin them? And why did she have to align herself with Grand-mère? Why wouldn't anyone take her part? Would she spend the rest of her life defending herself from attack? She pushed back from the table and swept out of the room before the tears could escape.

The door to her grandfather's study beckoned. It had been a refuge when she was growing up, a place where she felt unconditional acceptance. Alexandra's tears disappeared, replaced by a crushing weight. She was so weary, so drained.

She opened the study door and went in, her gaze traveling from the tall, book-filled shelves to her grandfather's wide, walnut desk. It looked exactly as it had in her childhood. If she closed her eyes, she could almost hear his deep voice barking orders for the day's work. Walking to the nearest bookcase, she saw the worn cover of his Bible. She pulled the book out of its place and went to a large leather chair near the cold fireplace, glad the room was warm enough that a fire was not necessary.

She slipped off her shoes and curled up in the chair, holding the large volume in her lap and wondering why it was not used more often by her relatives. She could not remember ever seeing Grand-mère read from a Bible. When Alexandra was a child, her mother had talked about her own parents' faith. What had happened to make Grand-mère turn from the faith that had once sustained her? Or had she merely pretended to believe to appease Grandpapa?

She opened the Bible with a sigh. Perhaps things would have turned out differently if this book had not been tucked away in his study.

Isaiah, the prophet. Not a very good place to start. Maybe she could find the verses about comforting the mournful. Underlined words stayed her hand: *"But Zion said, The Lord hath forsaken me, and my Lord hath forgotten me."*

The words resounded with her. If God really was there, He had forgotten all about her. But the underlining didn't stop there.

"Can a woman forget her sucking child, that she should not have compassion on the son of her womb? yea, they may forget, yet will I not forget thee. Behold, I have graven thee upon the palms of my hands; thy walls are continually before me."

The promise in the underlined verses was impossible to miss. She opened up her hand and looked at the palm. According to these words, God had written—no, *engraved*—her in the palms of His hands. A tear slipped down her cheek. Engraved in His hand. The truth was almost impossible to believe. Yet there it was. His answer to her complaint. God had not forgotten her after all.

Alexandra closed the book and slipped out of the chair to her knees. She steepled her hands and closed her eyes. Words seemed unnecessary as God's love filled the silent room. Her heart, her very soul, writhed as she confessed her doubt and sin. Then it was gone, and she knew. Christ had interceded for her. With boundless love, He had given His best for her. His blood had washed away her sin. The wonder of His truth washed over her, and peace settled on her shoulders. Never again would she have to wonder if He cared. She knew it with every fiber of her being.

Alexandra would have spent the rest of the afternoon in her grandfather's study if she hadn't heard someone calling her name. She rose with a contented sigh. She was a different person than the one who had sought solace here. When she opened the door, she came face-to-face with Aunt Patricia.

"What on earth have you been doing, Alexandra?"

She glanced back over her shoulder before answering. "I was talking to God."

A smile creased Aunt Patricia's face. She gave Alexandra a hug. "What a perfect thing to do on the Sabbath."

"I. . .I have been ignoring Him ever since Papa's death. But today He got my attention in the most wonderful way. Did you know our names are graven on His hand?"

Aunt Patricia laughed and hugged her again. "Of course. Isn't it wonderful?"

Alexandra nodded. "Were you looking for me?"

"Oh my, yes." Aunt Patricia stepped back. "I almost forgot. Young Sheffield has arrived as my mother predicted. He seems full of remorse and quite eager to see you."

A shrug lifted Alexandra's shoulders. "I am not sure he and I have anything to say to each other."

"I know he must have hurt your feelings terribly, Alexandra, but you cannot hold a grudge against him, not when you have so recently been reminded of God's grace. How many times do you think you have disappointed Him?"

Remorse filled her heart. "When you put it that way, I have to agree." Now it was Alexandra's turn to offer a hug. "It's disconcerting how quickly I can forget what I just learned."

"Yes, that is why we should seek out the company of other Christians. They help us stay accountable."

Alexandra's mouth turned up in a smile. "Thank you."

"That's quite all right, dear. Now go in there and visit that anxious young man."

When she opened the door to the parlor, Lowell's back was turned toward her. His head was bent as though he was depressed. She must have made some sound because he twisted around to face her.

She smiled, feeling God's peace inside her as warm and bright as a candelabra. "I'm so glad to see you, Lowell."

twenty

"The harvest is almost finished." Jeremiah looked over the fields with satisfaction. The white bolls of cotton had been picked, and most of them had been ginned to separate the seeds from the usable fibers. He strode to a nearby barn and pulled open the wide doors, waiting for Judah to catch up to him.

"It's hard for me to believe all you've managed to get done." Judah's voice was full of appreciation. "And it's something I can never repay."

Jeremiah rolled his eyes and flung a hand out to indicate the stacks of tightly packed bales. "We haven't turned all this into money yet."

"Jeremiah, Master Judah." Oren, the slave who had been so valuable to him for the past several weeks, walked over to them. "We's about to start piling the cotton into wagons."

"That's good." Jeremiah smiled at the man. "You've done a great job. I've been telling Judah how much help you've been."

"Yes." Judah leaned against the wall. "I am so pleased with all the work you've done."

A wide smile split the man's face. He bent the upper part of his body in a partial bow. "Thank you, sir. I was worried 'bout things for a while, but Jeremiah here, he got things working real smooth. He's been good to all us slaves. We would do anything for him, and you and the missus, o' course."

"Thank you, Oren. It was a real pleasure to work with you and the others." Jeremiah could feel Judah's surprised gaze on him. He shrugged. He hadn't done anything miraculous, just treated the slaves like men instead of property. He supposed he'd earned their respect because he'd worked right alongside them, refusing to quit until the work was done. It had been a

117

backbreaking but rewarding exercise. A part of him wished it was not over.

The sound of a wagon trundling toward them made Jeremiah step back. "How many loads do you think it will take, Oren?"

Oren looked at the wagon and then at the stacks of bales. "I guess we can get about a hun'erd bales to a load. And there's the two wagons." He squeezed his face tightly as he considered. "Mebbe three or four trips to town will do 'er."

Jeremiah nodded. "That's what I was thinking. It will take us half a day for each load, so we won't be done until tomorrow or maybe Wednesday." He turned to Judah. "What do you think about using the storehouse in the back of my new shipping office? That way we won't be forced to sell to the first captain who offers us a price."

Judah nodded. "A sound suggestion. What are you going to charge for storing the bales?"

"Nothing at all."

"Jeremiah, I cannot continue letting you shoulder all of my responsibility. You've done more than I ever dreamed. It's time to let me start repaying my debt."

"I've been thinking about that. . . ." Jeremiah let the words drift off.

"Don't tell me." Judah laughed so hard his shoulders shook. "You've got an idea."

Jeremiah joined him. It felt good to laugh. To enjoy the bounty of this day.

Oren looked from one to the other of them, a tentative smile on his face.

It took a few moments, but the laughter finally came to an end. Jeremiah clapped his friend on the shoulder. "Yes, I do. But why don't we let Oren get started working out here? I want to explain my idea to both you and Susannah at the same time."

He gathered up the slaves who would load and transport the cotton, explaining what needed to be done before leaving

Oren in charge. Then he and Judah walked back to the main house. "I cannot tell you how much I've enjoyed these days."

"You are a different man from the one I knew in New Orleans."

Jeremiah considered the statement as he helped Judah negotiate the steps to the front porch. "I feel different, too. It's almost like being closer to God to bring the crops to maturity and harvest them."

The two men went inside and found Susannah in the parlor, cutting out squares for a quilt. She glanced up as they entered. "What are the pair of you up to? You look as though you've been involved in some mischief."

Judah sat next to her on the sofa and leaned his crutches against the wall. "We were out checking the cotton, but Jeremiah says he has something he wants to talk to us about."

Jeremiah went to the fireplace and held his hands out toward the dancing flames. He closed his eyes and prayed for the right words to explain his hopes to these friends. If they agreed, he believed things would go more smoothly for all three of them, but he wanted more than anything to follow God's will. Taking a deep breath, he turned to the couple. "First of all, I'd like to say how much I appreciate your letting me work on the cotton harvest these past weeks. It has always been a dream of mine to farm, and you've helped me realize that dream."

Judah opened his mouth, but Jeremiah forestalled him with a shake of his head. "I don't want to get bogged down in compliments and comparisons this morning, so please hear me out. You did an excellent job getting the new office ready for business, Judah. I couldn't believe how much you accomplished in such a short time. The apartment upstairs still needs work, but I think it could be made livable, even for a couple."

He glanced toward his friends and let a smile bend his mouth upward. "I also purchased several acres behind the office that are currently vacant. My idea is to build a home on that property, one large enough to house the owner and his family. That way, he will be close to his family even when he's working. I don't think it will take long to build the house as there seems to be an abundance of capable workers in town. I am hoping it will be finished and the owner can take up residence before next autumn."

"I don't understand, Jeremiah." Susannah put down her mending and frowned at him. "You sound like you are not planning to stay here and run your shipping business."

Jeremiah nodded. "That's right. I have never enjoyed the business like my uncle does. I have already written to him telling him I didn't relish the idea of returning to the shipping industry and asking if he would consider allowing a young couple I know to join his business." Jeremiah reached into his pocket and pulled out a folded note. "He wrote back that he likes the idea of incorporating another family into LeGrand Shipping, and he is delighted to have a war hero for a business partner." He waited for the meaning of his words to sink in.

Susannah looked at her husband. "It's the answer to our prayers."

Judah looked at each of them, clearly torn. "I don't know. . . ."

A glance upward accompanied Jeremiah's prayer for the right words. "I know this will be a big change for you, so I'd like for you to take your time and discuss it thoroughly. If you have any doubts at all, we can talk it over beforehand."

It seemed to be the reassurance his friend needed. "I don't think there's any need for that." Judah glanced toward his wife and received a nod. "Susannah and I would be foolish to reject your offer." He picked up his crutches and pulled himself up. Leaning his weight against them, he held out his right hand.

Jeremiah crossed the distance to the sofa in two strides. He gripped Judah's hand firmly. "You don't know what this means to me."

Susannah stood up next to them. "You don't know what it means to us, either. I don't know why we didn't think of it ourselves. It makes so much sense. Your talent in running a plantation is obvious from the work you've managed to accomplish. And living in town is the perfect answer for me and Judah." She leaned up and placed a kiss on Jeremiah's cheek. "Sometimes I think you are an angel sent from God."

"Maybe not an angel." Judah put an arm around his wife. "But he does remind me of Abraham, who walked without question the path God set out before him."

While Jeremiah felt uncomfortable with their lavish praise, he did feel God's hand at work and could only praise Him for His loving guidance on all their lives.

twenty-one

Jeremiah's fingers tangled in the folds of his cravat. He seemed to have lost the ability to dress himself. He could not be nervous about hosting his first party as the owner of Magnolia Plantation. His gaze fell on the folded papers he and Judah had signed to formalize their exchange and thanked God for working things out to both their benefits over the past month.

Someone knocked at the door to the master bedroom.

"I'll be down in a few minutes." He walked over and jerked the door open as he spoke, expecting that Susannah had sent someone to hustle him downstairs.

He was not surprised to find Ezekiel standing there. "I come to see if you need help, master." The weathered face of the former slave whom he now employed as a butler/valet focused at a point somewhere behind him.

Jeremiah stepped back. "Ezekiel, haven't I asked you not to call me master? You are a free man now. I am your employer. The Lord is your only Master."

"Yessir, mas—I mean Mister Jeremiah." A smile of pleasure split the man's face. "I guess I'm het up over all the excitement downstairs. What with Miss Susannah worrying 'bout you getting downstairs before yore guests start arriving. . ."

"If you can, help me with this cravat. I can't seem to make the silly thing cooperate." He turned back to the mirror and tugged on his shirt collars, which were beginning to droop a little.

Ezekiel clucked his tongue. "Let me see that."

Jeremiah sighed and raised his chin.

It only took a moment or two before Ezekiel stepped back. "Is that better?"

A glance in the mirror confirmed that he had chosen his

valet well. "Perfect. I don't know what I'd do without you, Ezekiel."

The other man chuckled. He picked up the frock coat lying across Jeremiah's bed and held it up. "It's good to have a little help here and there."

Jeremiah eased his arms into the coat and waited while Ezekiel smoothed the material over his shoulders. "I feel like a trussed up chicken."

Ezekiel shook his head. "You look nice. Like the gentleman you are. Now why don't you get on downstairs before Miss Susannah comes up here to find you."

The look that passed between them was full of understanding. All the people working for him at Magnolia Plantation knew Jeremiah did not relish social gatherings. He headed toward the entrance hall with a sigh and prayed the evening would end quickly.

Judah was waiting for him at the foot of the stairs. "Susannah was beginning to fear you weren't going to be here in time to greet your guests."

"Where is your lovely wife?" He glanced around him. Candles and flowers seemed to fill every corner and surface of the vestibule, but he saw no sign of Susannah.

"She's gone to see about a trunk of items your housekeeper has collected for shipment to our apart—"

"If I never move again it will be too soon." Susannah's voice interrupted him. She moved gracefully toward them, her blond curls bobbing as she shook her head. "I never realized how much we had accumulated since moving here. And I don't know where we're going to put it until our new house is finished."

Jeremiah bowed to her. "You are most welcome to store everything here until you have more room. I know you and Judah must be cramped in your rooms above the shipping office."

"Nonsense." She reached up and patted his cheek. "I've no doubt you will soon settle down with a wife and family and will need every inch of space for them."

He grimaced. "Don't be so certain. I am content with things as they are for now."

Judah winked at him. "Susannah can't help herself. She's a born matchmaker."

The diminutive woman smiled toward her husband. "Can I help wanting others to experience the happiness we have?"

The loving look they shared made Jeremiah feel like an outsider. Would he ever find a woman to share his life? The arrival of the first guests ended his speculation. He waited while Judah performed the introductions, spoke to the couple briefly, and gestured toward the ballroom as the next visitors entered.

He recognized many of the guests from church, including the pastor and Mr. and Mrs. Sheffield, who arrived with their son, Lowell. But there were others he had never met previously. There was a pause in the flow of guests after the arrival of one such family.

"I cannot believe the Osbournes came." Judah leaned against the oak balustrade behind him.

Susannah frowned at him. "Why wouldn't they come? I made sure to include them. I am sorry their oldest daughter ran away from home, but that is no reason to exclude the rest of the family. And their youngest girl, Felicity, is of marriageable age."

"I didn't say you should not have invited them." Judah straightened and stepped toward his wife. Jeremiah could not help but compare his friend's animation and energy against the bitterness and defeat that had once ruled Judah. Running the shipping business in town had given his friend a reason to believe in himself once more. "I am just surprised they ventured out. This is the first party they've attended since the scandal became common knowledge."

The rest of the conversation was cut off as the front door opened once more for the Tanner family. The matriarch, Mrs. Tanner, entered first, her cane tapping the marble floor. She was followed by the rest of the family—John and Patricia Bass, Mrs. Lewis, and finally the beautiful Alexandra Lewis. Jeremiah found himself unable to tear his eyes away from her. She looked so elegant in her finery, her dark hair piled high on her head, her eyes glowing in the reflected light of the candles.

"Have the Sheffields already arrived?" Mrs. Tanner's question brought his attention back to her.

"Yes, ma'am." He bowed over her hand even though her question cut through him like a sword thrust. "Welcome to Magnolia. I hope you and your family enjoy yourselves this evening."

"That remains to be seen." She moved away, followed by her daughter and son-in-law.

Alexandra's mother was next, her whispered greeting barely reaching his ears before she followed her relatives into the ballroom.

Alexandra dropped a curtsy and held out her hand, encased in a black glove. As Jeremiah took it, he wished he could think of something witty to say. Something that would impress her. But his brain turned to mush. He barely managed to get out the necessary greeting before watching her enter the ballroom.

"I imagine most everyone has arrived." Susannah held a hand out to her husband. "Let's join them in the ballroom."

The orchestra had been playing for some time now, and the ballroom floor had become crowded with couples of all ages. His gaze rested on a lone young woman who stood a little apart from the rest of the young, single ladies hoping to be partnered for the next dance. He recognized her as Miss Osbourne, the girl whose older sister had caused a scandal. Perhaps he should ask her to dance.

He headed toward her but was cut off by a group of talkative debutantes who moved in her direction. Miss Osbourne looked up at their approach, an expression of hope on her face. One of the young women pointed at her and giggled, another put a hand to her mouth, while the third girl simply turned her face away. It was the cut direct. His heart went out to her. Another innocent condemned by the narrow dictates of local society.

Miss Osbourne's face crumpled, and she ran toward the nearest exit which he knew led to the library. He started to follow her, wanting to reassure her, but before he could take a single step, someone brushed past him. The scent of lemons filled the air. Alexandra Lewis. She hurried out the same door Miss Osbourne had taken. Was she intent on comforting the girl? His heart warmed. What better person to speak to her than someone who had endured a similar experience? He turned back to the ballroom and assumed his responsibilities as host.

Jeremiah smiled and made his way around the room, speaking to everyone and answering whatever questions came his way. Yes, he had freed his slaves. Yes, he had supplied land and seed for those eager to support themselves, as well as hiring many of the former slaves to help him on the plantation. No, he had no fear of being murdered in his own bed. He made it a point to speak to Mr. and Mrs. Osbourne, hoping his actions would be copied by his other guests.

He was about to go in search of Miss Osbourne and Alexandra when they returned to the ballroom. Alexandra beckoned toward Lowell Sheffield, who moved toward her. Even though he was several feet away, Jeremiah could hear her as she introduced her beau to the shy young woman at her side. Lowell dutifully asked the girl to dance, and the pair of them left Alexandra standing alone.

A desire to thank Alexandra for her thoughtfulness overwhelmed him, and he moved toward her. "May I have this dance?"

Her dark gaze met his own. "I am flattered, sir."

Jeremiah led her to the center of the room as the orchestra began playing a minuet. He had to concentrate on the steps and therefore did not get to speak his mind. But as soon as the music died away, he took her by the arm. "I'd like a word with you if you have a moment."

Color rose in her cheeks, but she nodded and allowed him to lead her through one of the arched doorways onto the wide balcony outside.

"What did you wish to say to me?" Even though there was little light out here, he could see that her shoulders were squared and her chin was high.

"I am very impressed that you left the party to comfort Miss Osbourne." He wished he could see the expression on her face as she absorbed his words. But all he could see was the shrug of her shoulders.

"Jeremiah, you are the one who taught me to reach out to others when they are hurting. How could I do less for that poor young woman than you did for me? She just needed someone to remind her of God's love."

Her lemony perfume enveloped him once again, making him think of warm breezes and long summer afternoons. He couldn't stop himself from leaning toward her. She was so sweet, so sincere in her explanation. Even though he would never have wished such pain on her, he could see how much maturity it had brought her. She was no longer the self-centered girl he had met in Natchez Under-the-Hill. And he found himself falling in love with the young woman she had become.

His heart pounded. Falling in love? With Alexandra Lewis? He cleared his throat and tried to marshal his thoughts. "Alexandra. . .I—"

"Alexandra, there you are." Light seemed to flood their corner of the balcony as Lowell pulled back a curtain and stepped toward them. "Your grandmother told me to come find you. She wants to see us dancing together."

Jeremiah could not think of a way to prevent the young man from inserting himself between them. He watched as she smiled up at Lowell. Was that relief on her face? Or were the shadows playing tricks with him? Yet she never looked back as Sheffield led her to the ballroom.

And why should she? Her future had already been set for

her. Her kindness this evening had probably been nothing more than a performance for the benefit of Lowell and his family. Why else would she choose to return with him to the dancing?

He was a fool for thinking she had changed. Without God's intervention, she would never be anything more than a shallow girl intent on securing her place in local society.

twenty-two

Sadness filled Alexandra as Lowell helped her into his carriage. She glanced back at Jeremiah LeGrand, so tall and straight, standing alone on the steps of the church. Last night's party did not appear to have endeared him to the townspeople. He looked like a boulder in a rushing stream, untouched by the men and women who brushed past him.

Lowell climbed up next to her and grabbed the reins. "What are you looking at?"

She turned and offered him a smile. "Nothing. I was just wondering if what I heard about Jeremiah LeGrand was true. Has he really bought Magnolia Plantation?"

"Yes. It's a disgrace. Pa says he's making a mockery of all the other planters. Did you know he's freed all of his slaves?" Lowell slapped the reins. "Claims he can make his plantation work by paying his laborers and allowing them to grow their own crops." Alexandra did not much care for the sneer he wore as he continued. "Several of our neighbors say it's going to lead to rebellion and maybe worse. We've instructed our overseers to report any suspicious activities among our own slaves."

Alexandra looked at the set face of the man beside her. "Is there any chance Mr. LeGrand is right? Slavery seems so terrible to me."

"Slavery is not terrible. It's been around for a long time. It's a biblical concept. Even the Jews used slaves to get their work done. In more than one place, the Bible warns slaves to work hard for their masters. Paul said they should do their best work like they are working for the Lord."

"But what about the farmer who paid wages to his workers in Jesus' parable?"

"You don't understand the least thing on this subject, Alexandra. If I set my slaves free, they wouldn't be able to fend for themselves. They would probably end up dead from starvation or become criminals who rob others of what they have."

Alexandra wanted to argue they could be taught skills. On her grandmother's plantation, many of the slaves worked as carpenters, blacksmiths, and bricklayers. They even had a cabinetmaker. Obviously these men were skilled. But Lowell did not give her a chance as he warmed up to his theme.

"I can't agree with people who mistreat their slaves, but as long as we feed and clothe them, they are better off than if they were free and had to deal with all the problems Pa and I have to solve. They're much like little children, happier when they are told where to go and what to do. In turn, their work makes it possible to produce the cotton the rest of the world wants. Without slaves, I would not be able to turn a profit."

"But what if Mr. LeGrand teaches his slaves a trade? Wouldn't that be a better solution for them and for him?"

The glance Lowell tossed at her was full of scorn. "I suppose it speaks well of your tender heart to be so concerned with the welfare of others, but you should leave such things to men."

Disbelief flashed through Alexandra. In previous days, she might have lashed out at Lowell for his attitude, but those days were gone. Her faith would not let her continue challenging Lowell's stance. She would pray for a change of heart for the man sitting beside her. Lowell was an intelligent, well-educated man. Surely he would eventually be open to new ideas.

A long, mournful whistle gained her attention. "That sounds like a steamboat." She put a hand on Lowell's arm. "Can we go to the waterfront and watch it come in?"

He glanced down at her hand and then into her eyes. She could tell by his gaze that Lowell was smitten. Alexandra's cheeks warmed at the message she read in his hazel eyes. She removed her hand as if it had been burned.

"Of course, I'll take you if you think your family won't mind."

Alexandra considered. "We won't stay long. I love seeing the paddlewheels churning through the water, and the people are so interesting."

"Pa says most of them are riffraff and wastrels looking for an easy life."

The flush drained out of her cheeks. "Lowell"—she could not keep the disappointment from her voice—"I cannot believe you said that. Many of those people have sold everything they own for passage here. They deserve our sympathy, not our scorn."

He didn't answer her as he maneuvered the carriage around to comply with her request, but the set of his chin told her he was not happy with her point of view. Another difference.

Alexandra was beginning to wonder if they had anything in common. They should have seen eye-to-eye on any number of topics, but the more they were together, the more she realized they did not. It was ironic. Lowell would probably ask for her hand in marriage in the next few days, but she wanted more than anything to tell him they would not suit.

He guided the carriage to the edge of a bluff between a pair of towering, leafless oak trees. The wind pulled at her scarf and cloak, burning her cheeks as it whipped around them. The discomfort disappeared, however, when she spotted the twin chimneys of the steamship coming around the bend. "Look, there it is."

"Careful, Alexandra." Lowell jumped down from the carriage and looped the reins around one of the lower limbs of the tree on his side of the carriage. He strode around to her side and held his arms up.

Alexandra put a hand in one of his, expecting him to steady her as she dismounted. Instead, he circled her waist with both hands and lifted her out of her seat, swinging her around before he allowed her feet to touch the ground.

She was caught off guard by his move and a nervous giggle tried to escape from her throat. Not wishing to encourage his behavior, she clamped her lips together. She stepped away from him and faced the river. "Can you read the boat's name?"

"No." Lowell's voice sounded choked, but Alexandra refused to turn around. "I have something more interesting to watch."

"Really, what's that?" She glanced back over her shoulder for a moment. If his gaze had been ardent before, it was a raging fire now. A fire that threatened to consume her. She had to face him or risk losing control of the situation.

"You are so beautiful, Alexandra."

It was too soon. She wasn't ready. She didn't have her answer ready. She had to stop him from going further. "You are very sweet, Lowell, but I think you were right after all. We need to get back home. Everyone will be sitting down to dinner, and they'll wonder where I am." She met his gaze, hoping he would read the plea in hers.

A long moment of silence stretched between them. His breathing was labored, as if he'd run all the way up the bluff instead of driving. His gaze dropped to her mouth. Alexandra knew he was about to embrace her. What should she do? Let him have his way?

She felt his hands on her shoulders, pulling her closer. Her heart was thumping like an Indian drum. But was the feeling coursing through her anticipation or dread?

His eyes drifted closed, and he pursed his lips, making her want to giggle once more. He looked like nothing so much as a hooked fish. At the last minute she turned her head and his lips landed somewhere near the base of her ear.

"Lowell, stop." She pushed him away.

Ever the gentleman, Lowell allowed her to put some distance between them. "Alexandra, I have something I'd like to ask you about."

"Not now, Lowell. There's no time." She scrambled back

into the carriage without any help, drew her cloak around her shoulders, and tapped her foot. "I have to get home."

He sighed and nodded. "Have it your way, Alexandra. But this cannot wait forever."

She chattered about every subject that came to mind all the way home, hardly allowing Lowell to insert a comment. She started with the sermon—an uplifting message based on Psalm 33—and ended with a one-sided discussion on the advantages of statehood. By the time they arrived at the house, she was winded.

Lowell looked confused. She could understand why. She felt the same way. That was why she had to postpone his proposal. She needed to pray for an answer about what to do.

Grand-mère still expected her to marry. Mama was counting on her to provide a home through an advantageous union. But could she truthfully repeat the oaths that would bind her to Lowell for the rest of their lives? Could she promise to honor and obey him? What about the differences that were becoming more obvious with each day that passed?

On the other hand, Lowell had decided to proceed with his courtship despite the scandal revealed during Dorcas's visit. But his loyalty was only a result of his family's respect for her grandmother's wealth. If she found herself as poor as she'd been in Nashville, she had no doubt Lowell would disappear.

So she smiled and thanked him for escorting her home. Then she left him standing on the porch and went inside to have Sunday dinner with her family. Perhaps she would figure out what to do before too much longer.

twenty-three

Going to town felt like a terrible waste of time. Jeremiah had begun working with the blacksmith, a burly former slave who now received a wage for his craft. The horses and mules needed to be reshod, the plows needed to be sharpened and straightened, and rusty scythes needed to be replaced. The planting season was almost upon them, and Jeremiah was far from prepared.

But he could not turn down the request from his friends. Susannah wanted to show off the improvements they'd made to the building. Judah wanted his opinion on a problem with a shipment. And both accused him of becoming a hermit. So he left the blacksmith with detailed instructions, saddled his horse, and rode to town. Perhaps he would get back before sunset and do a little work.

Jeremiah arrived at the shipping office before mid-morning. The scene inside was hectic, with boat captains, farmers, and planters all vying for Judah's attention. His friend was methodical in his work, however, proving he was the right choice for this job. After haggling over prices, he posted a large sign with the day's rate for the available commodities and began to take orders and set up delivery dates and times.

The office eventually emptied out, and Judah sat back with a long sigh. "I can't believe I let you talk me into this work."

Jeremiah laughed. "I can't believe you are so good at it. My uncle had better watch out, or you'll soon own his whole company."

The smile on Judah's face was as wide as the river outside. He looked content. "I have a confession to make though. I don't really have a problem for you to help with."

"I'm not surprised, not after watching you this morning.

You are so much more competent than I ever was. You could probably teach me a thing or two."

Judah grabbed his crutches and stood up. "Let's go upstairs. I'm certain Susannah has lunch ready by now. Then I want to take you down to the docks. There's a group down there I think you'll be interested in seeing."

"What kind of group?" Jeremiah waited while Judah locked the office door.

"You'll see."

The two men climbed the narrow staircase that led to the renovated apartment above the office and joined Susannah in the dining room. She was as full of energy as ever, pointing out all the items she'd purchased since his last visit and sharing her plans for flower and vegetable gardens as soon as their new house was completed. The talk between them was lively and fun. Jeremiah had forgotten what it was like to take his meals with friends. Maybe he was getting too reclusive.

"Are you ready, dear?" asked Judah when they finished eating.

Susannah pushed back from the table and nodded. "The carriage should be waiting." She winked at her husband. "You didn't tell him, did you?"

"Not a word."

"Hey." Jeremiah raised a hand. "The two of you are talking like I'm in another room. I'm right here."

Susannah glanced in his direction, a sly smile on her face. "So you are. Let's get our cloaks and be on our way."

The road that separated Natchez Under-the-Hill from the main part of town was steep but not difficult to negotiate. Jeremiah looked out of the window at the line of dugout canoes, keelboats, and steamboats vying for space along the banks of the river. He had forgotten how noisy it was, the mix of languages and accents, the shouts of vendors, and the sweet chorus of familiar hymns.

Hymns? Who would be singing hymns down here? He turned a startled glance toward his hosts, whose faces held identical, knowing smiles.

The carriage drew to a halt, and Jeremiah pushed the door open, jumping out before the coachman had time to let down the step. Ignoring his friends, he walked toward the sound of the singing.

" 'Through many dangers, toils, and snares. . .' "

His steps hastened. He rounded a corner. A crowd of immigrants, mostly children, lifted their voices to praise God. The sound filled the very air around him, almost angelic in its power and beauty. He could not resist joining them, adding his baritone to the wonderful mix of voices. When the last note drifted out over the surface of the water, he finally looked to the front to see who was leading this group. A trio of ladies stood together, dressed in fancy cloaks and hats.

His mouth dropped open. Alexandra? Was this the young woman he'd judged to be too conscious of her social standing? Too caught up in worldly matters? Yes, he'd seen a change in her during church services, but Jeremiah had never dreamed she could have come so far as to spend her time here. Yet there she stood, her aunt on one side, her mother on the other. She leaned over and whispered something to her mother, who nodded.

"Thank you so much for joining us." Alexandra's voice was not loud, but it carried well, even out here in the open. "It surely pleased God to hear our voices joined in praise. We have one other song that I think most of you will have heard. After that, please follow us to the green house down to your right where we will have a warm meal for everyone."

Her mother began singing first. " 'Eternal depth of love divine, in Jesus, God with us, displayed.' "

Alexandra and her aunt added their voices, and soon the crowd was singing again. He heard Susannah's soprano and Judah's bass behind him, but his attention centered on the girl who stood so calmly up front and brought hope to these tired and weary people.

The woman who had dismissed him as nothing more

than a servant was now ministering to those less fortunate than she, while treating them with the same love Christ would have shown. She saw souls in need, not servants to meet her needs. How could he do anything except love her? He had always found Alexandra devastatingly beautiful, but now she had exceeded any notions he once held of the ideal wife.

As soon as the song was finished, he eased his way through the dispersing crowd. He wanted—no needed—to talk to her. "Alexandra!"

Her head turned, and their gazes met. Something passed between them, something wordless, spiritual, and loving. It was as though their souls embraced. Her eyes widened, and he knew she felt it, too. He reached her side and held out an arm.

She placed her hand on it. "Mr. LeGrand, you are looking well. Have you come to help us distribute food and blankets?"

He shook his head. . .then nodded.

Alexandra laughed. "Well, which is it? Yes or no?"

He swallowed hard. "I came with Judah and his wife. They didn't tell me you would be here."

Her velvet brown eyes darkened. "I don't know how I'm to take that. Are you saying you would not have come if you'd known?"

Jeremiah felt tongue-tied. He wasn't very adept at talking to women, but he'd never been quite this abysmal. "Not at all." He decided to try another tack. "Your singing was wonderful. I know the people here were blessed by it. You are providing them with the hope they need to continue their journeys."

A blush rose in her cheeks, and she broke eye contact. "It was my aunt's idea. She is so eager to share God's love. All I do is help where I can."

They were walking amongst the immigrants and dockworkers now, and he glanced around at the happy faces. "Don't diminish your contribution. Whenever you give of your time and the talents God has graced you with, you are doing His will, walking in the path He set for you."

Jeremiah would have continued, but they arrived at the house where the food would be handed out.

Alexandra broke away from him with a smile of thanks. "I have to go help the others. Thank you for escorting me here."

He bowed and let her be swept away from him. But he stayed to help, handing out what they had prepared. From time to time, he found himself standing close to her. But then they were separated once again. He hoped to escort her and her mother and aunt back to Tanner Plantation, but Susannah and Judah dragged him away before the women were ready to depart.

"Did you enjoy yourself this afternoon?" Susannah asked as the carriage climbed back up the hill.

"It was one of the best days I've had since I came to Natchez."

Judah groaned.

His wife laughed. "I told my husband you were in love with Alexandra Lewis. He didn't believe me. But I've known it for a long time now."

Heat climbed up Jeremiah's throat. How was it that Susannah had understood what he had been too blind to see? Women just seemed to know these things. What about Alexandra? How long had she known? "She is a fascinating young lady."

Judah wrapped his hand around his wife's. "Maybe so, but she is not nearly as fascinating nor as wise as the beauty I am married to."

"How can I argue with that statement?" Jeremiah was glad to have the attention removed from him. "Your wife is indeed a woman of integrity and charm, even if she is a little devious at times."

All three of them laughed and then began to talk of the people they had met that day. The sun was beginning to set by the time they made it back to the shipping office.

Even though they pressed him to stay for a while, Jeremiah refused. He had a lot to think and pray over this evening, and he needed solitude to do it.

twenty-four

Dorcas Montgomery was on her way back to Nashville. Grand-mère had delivered the information with relish. "Now there's no reason not to bring young Sheffield to the point."

Alexandra swallowed hard. "I'm not sure that's going to work." They were sitting in the parlor, taking tea. At least they didn't have any visitors. Yet.

"Don't start that nonsense again, girl." Her grandmother slapped the arm of her chair. "You will smile prettily and say yes when he asks for your hand in marriage. If you don't, you will invite my extreme displeasure."

"Come, now." Aunt Patricia's tones were as phlegmatic as ever. "It's not as if you can put Beatrice and Alexandra out of your home."

Alexandra cast a thankful glance in her aunt's direction. "I promise to work very hard, Grand-mère. I don't like being a burden to you, but I don't want to link my future with a man I do not love."

"Love!" Her grandmother spat the word. "Love is for commoners. You have a duty to your family. To all the children you will one day have. A duty you—will—not—forsake." The last three words were said with such emphasis that Alexandra winced.

Before she could answer, however, the door opened, and the subject of their argument was announced. Lowell looked very fine, dressed in a cropped riding coat, his dark breeches tucked into polished black boots. He still held his hat and gloves in one hand but gave them to the maid before entering the room. "Good afternoon, ladies." He bowed to them and advanced toward Alexandra's grandmother. "You are looking very well, Mrs. Tanner."

"Thank you, Mr. Sheffield." She grabbed her cane. "Help me up, young man. I trust you won't be too disappointed to learn my daughter and I have business to see to upstairs."

Alexandra rose, too, but her grandmother shook her head. "You should stay here and entertain our guest."

Wishing the floor would swallow her up, Alexandra returned to her seat and watched as both of her relatives deserted her.

Lowell did not sit down as she expected. Instead, he took a turn about the room. "Alexandra, I'm sure you know why I've come today." He turned toward her, an expectant look on his charming features.

She leaned back against her chair and wished she'd thought to bring her fan to the parlor. "I. . .I suppose you wanted to see me."

He came to sit next to her on the sofa and reached for her hands. "Yes, but I have a very specific reason for doing so this afternoon." His palms were damp and cold, once again reminding her of a fish.

How could she ever say yes to him? Yet how could she say no? Alexandra withdrew her hands from his grasp and pushed herself up. She walked to the piano in one corner of the room and ran a finger across the keys. The sound was forlorn, echoing the sadness in her heart. She turned around and practically buried her nose in Lowell's chest.

He took a step back and captured her hands once again. Then he sank to one knee. "Alexandra Lewis, I adore you. Ever since you came back to Natchez, you have captured my imagination, my every waking thought. You are the perfect woman to become my wife. You will add charm and beauty to my home. Please say you'll marry me."

As proposals went, she supposed it was a good one. Alexandra was flattered by his declaration, but her heart was not touched. Everything in her screamed for escape. But Lowell was a good man, and she was supposed to obey her mother. Although the commandments did not mention grandparents, she felt that was a minor point. Grand-mère was providing for her and should be accorded the same respect. Her heart thumped unpleasantly. "Yes."

Lowell looked stunned for a moment, but then he recovered. He stood up and swept her into his embrace. "Thank you, dearest." He pulled away, bent at the waist, and pressed a fervent kiss on her hand. "You've made me the happiest of men."

Alexandra stared at the ruffle on his shirt, unable to relax. What had she done?

twenty-five

The local newspaper had been folded next to Jeremiah's breakfast plate. He removed the domed cover to display a hearty breakfast of eggs, sausage, grits, and biscuits. After saying grace, he dug in and opened the paper to read the headlines. His eyes swept past a discussion of the evils of statehood and landed on an announcement.

His fork clattered to the table. He grabbed the paper and looked more closely. The words swam before his gaze. It could not be. But there it was in black-and-white. Alexandra Lewis had accepted a proposal from Lowell Sheffield. The woman he loved was in love with someone else. His heart shattered. The room darkened around him.

He looked again at the date. They were to be married in a month's time, at the end of April. Why the unseemly rush? Not that he would hesitate if he had secured her agreement. In fact, he would have pressed for an even earlier date. Lowell probably realized as well as he did that many men would like to call Alexandra theirs.

He threw the paper down on the table and pushed his chair back. His stomach roiled. He would never be able to finish his breakfast. The sustenance he needed could only come from turning to his Master. God would lend him wisdom and strength as He always had.

❧

Jeremiah saw Alexandra again at church the following Sunday. He thought he was prepared for the pain, but seeing young Sheffield standing so near her took his breath away.

Susannah and Judah stayed close to him, their expressions full of sympathy and sadness.

"You're a better man than he is." Judah's whisper took his

attention away from Alexandra.

He shrugged and pushed his hands down into his pockets as they left the church.

"My husband is right, you know." Susannah's voice exposed her concern. "She is making a bad decision. You should go to her, tell her how you feel—"

"Stop right there." Jeremiah knew they meant their words for the best, but if they continued, he might lose his sanity and run screaming down the street. "I will be fine. She will be fine. I'm certain she is following God's lead. Now let me go and congratulate them."

He strode away from them to face the couple. "Let me add my best wishes to those of the rest of the town."

Alexandra looked up at him, her eyes dark and fathomless. For a moment he thought he saw panic in their depths, but it must have been his imagination. "Thank you, Mr. LeGrand." Her smile was as bright as the first rays of the rising sun. "I trust you will be able to attend our wedding. My grandmother is planning the ceremony. We're inviting family and all of our friends."

Pain swept through him at her words, and he realized that he'd been hoping the betrothal announcement was a mistake. Or perhaps that Alexandra needed to be rescued from her overbearing grandmother. But she seemed to have embraced a future as the wife of Lowell Sheffield, a man who was his exact opposite.

This then was the real Alexandra Lewis. The woman he thought he'd seen glimpses of, the one he was in love with, must be a figment of his imagination. "I thought you were someone different, but I was obviously mistaken." He let his gaze sweep from her dark, perfectly coiffed curls to the tips of her pointed leather boots. She was no more than an empty-headed girl eager to enjoy the luxuries of her station. "I'm sure it will be everything you plan and exactly what you deserve."

He clamped his jaws shut when he saw the tiny frown between her brows. What was it about this woman that affected him so? Shame replaced his disgust at her choice. Why had he ever thought someone like Alexandra Lewis could change?

When did I become so harsh?

Sheffield put a possessive arm around her waist and sent a pointed gaze in his direction. "Did Mr. LeGrand say something to disturb you, my dear?"

She shook her head and turned to the next person in line.

Jeremiah realized he'd been dismissed. Without another word, he retrieved his horse, climbed into the saddle, and cantered back to the plantation. Once there, he threw himself into his usual chores with determination. Perhaps he could work himself free of the shame and regret eating at him.

❧

Alexandra ran up the stairs to her room and threw herself across her bed. Tears soaked her pillow, the same tears that had threatened ever since Jeremiah's scornful remarks after church this morning. He was right, of course. She was nothing but a shallow, spineless mouse who could not stand up for what she knew was right.

Some time later, when her tears were exhausted, a knock on her door made Alexandra sit up. "Come in."

Her mother peeked around the edge of the door. "Am I disturbing you, dear?"

Alexandra slid off her bed and rubbed at her hot eyes. "N–no."

"Oh, my darling daughter." Her mother stepped inside, closed the door behind her, and held out her arms. "Come here and tell me all about it."

With a sob, Alexandra complied, falling into her mother's embrace. She had only thought the tears were dried up. They gushed from some vast well inside her and slipped around the corners of her eyes. She felt like a child as her mother stroked her back and murmured comforting words in her ear. After all they had been through, it seemed their relationship had come full circle.

Alexandra finally pulled away, sniffing.

Mama pulled a handkerchief from the pocket of her skirt and patted her daughter's wet cheeks with it. Then she looped her arm through one of Alexandra's and led her to a chair. "Sit down and let's see if we can sort this out."

Alexandra took a deep breath, still feeling the hitch in her chest from all the crying she'd done. She watched as her mother pulled another chair around to face her. "I don't know what to say."

Her mother raised an eyebrow at her. "Let's start with the problem that is making you cry your heart out. This is a very special time in your life. A time when you should be happy and excited, looking forward to your nuptials and setting up your own household."

"I know. And I am happy. It's just that. . .just that I don't want to be shallow and uncaring." She stopped to consider her words. "I have only recently realized what it means to be a Christian. I want to do the Lord's work."

Her mother tilted her head. "And you don't think you can do that once you marry Lowell?"

Alexandra sighed. How could she explain the problem without exposing the real reason for her sorrow? Jeremiah's pointed words had pierced her deeply. Every line of his face had screamed disdain. She shouldn't care. He was practically a stranger, but somehow she wanted to earn his approbation. She wanted to see his blue eyes glow with appreciation the way they had last week when she'd seen him on the riverfront. It mattered more to her than she could have ever imagined.

Knowing she could not give her mother the real reason for her tears, she finally settled on something that would be understood. "Lowell and I don't always see eye-to-eye on matters."

"Oh." Her mother dragged the syllable out. "So you've had a tiff with your betrothed?"

"No. Lowell is very understanding, but he doesn't think I should worry about things like business and commerce."

"Alexandra, when have you ever cared about such things?"

She looked across at her mother, unable to argue the point. Mama was right. She had never cared about the topics men seemed to spend so much time discussing. Never wondered about slavery or politics. She had always focused on clothes and parties, flirting and gossip.

But her tongue was tied by her inability to fully reveal what was in her heart. She could hardly admit to Mama her feelings for a man to whom she was not betrothed. So she shook her head and twisted the handkerchief she was still holding. "I don't know."

"Well then, I guess we'll have to put it down to youthful dithering." Her mother sighed. "Perhaps your father and I did not raise you as we should have. My mother certainly thinks we allowed you too much freedom."

Too much freedom? When she couldn't even choose her own husband? She had no freedom at all. But now was not the time to make a complaint. Now was the time to do her duty for her family. "Don't worry." She turned to face her mother. "I won't let you down, Mama."

And she would not. Her mother was counting on her to make an advantageous marriage. "Everything is all right. Thank you for coming to talk to me. I'm feeling better now." Putting on her best smile, she pushed aside her doubts and her feelings for Jeremiah LeGrand.

Her mother stared at her for a few moments before nodding. "Just remember how much you've dreamed of having a husband and a home of your own. Lowell is the answer to your prayers." She stood up, gave Alexandra one last hug, and left her alone.

Even if her own life was falling apart, Alexandra was comforted to see her mother beginning to resume her life. For a while, she had thought Mama would never recover from Papa's death. At least that fear had proved to be groundless.

Perhaps her fears that she was marrying the wrong man would also turn out to be groundless.

twenty-six

Jeremiah wiped sweat from his brow and shaded his eyes against the sun. A carriage and a pair of men on horses were riding up the lane toward his home. The gatekeeper, one of the freed slaves, came running to him. "Master Jeremiah, you got some fancy visitors comin' to see you."

He dropped the sledgehammer he'd been using to pound new fence posts into the ground. "Mark, didn't I tell you to stop calling me master?"

"Yessir. I'm sorry." The young man dug a toe in the ground.

Jeremiah put a hand on his shoulder. "It's okay. Now tell me what the men said."

Mark's eyes widened. "They said fo' me to come git you and tell you they was comin'."

He squeezed the boy's shoulder. "Okay, you've done what they asked. Now go on back to the gatehouse."

The young man, boy really, ran off.

Jeremiah walked to the well and raised a bucket of cool water, using it to wash his face and hands. Then he strode to the house, unrolling his sleeves as he walked. Too bad he didn't have time to change into fresh clothing, but it would be rude to keep his guests waiting that long.

He stopped to tell the cook to prepare scones and coffee before going to meet the men in his parlor. The tentative smile on his face disappeared when he saw Mr. Sheffield and his son, Lowell, standing to one side of the parlor, apparently discussing some divisive matter. A stocky, gray-haired man was staring into the fireplace. Randolph Fournier. Jeremiah recognized the man although he did not know him well. "What can I do for you gentlemen?"

Mr. Sheffield started as if Jeremiah had shot at him. Lowell shuffled his feet and looked at the floor. Mr. Fournier turned around and sketched a shallow bow before clearing his throat. "We've come on a very serious errand, I'm afraid."

The housekeeper entered the room with the tray he had ordered. Jeremiah thanked her and invited his guests to sit down. None of them spoke until she left the room.

Pouring the coffee carefully, he passed the brimming cups to each of them. "Please forgive my clumsiness. I am an awkward host."

Mr. Fournier took a sip from his cup, made a face, and set it down. "Your manners, or the lack of them, are not the reason we're here."

Mr. Sheffield turned down the coffee but took one of the scones from the tray. "Yes, we have heard a troubling rumor about how you're running this place. But instead of condemning you outright, we came to find out the truth of the matter."

Sitting back against the sofa, Jeremiah forced his fists to relax. He understood exactly why these men were here. They were going to try to force him to follow their rules. He crossed his arms over his chest. "Go ahead."

This time, Lowell spoke up. "Is it true you are paying your slaves—"

"Former slaves."

Lowell grimaced at the interruption. "Are you paying them for the crops they are raising on your land?"

"Yes." Jeremiah did not elaborate. The way he saw it, these men had no right to question the way he ran things at Magnolia. And if they thought they could stop him from doing what he thought was right, they would soon learn their mistake. He would never try to tell any of them how to run their estates, and he expected the same consideration from them.

"Preposterous." Mr. Fournier raised a white handkerchief to his nose and sniffed. "You come in here from who knows where and stir things up with your radical ideas. You may not realize how much trouble you're causing, but the whole town is in an uproar. Even the slaves. Don't think they haven't learned about what you've done. It's a wonder we haven't all been murdered in our beds. You have put all of us in danger. We will not allow anarchy to rule here."

"Mr. Fournier, Mr. Sheffield, Lowell"—he nodded to each man as he spoke their names, praying for temperance— "while I realize each of you is an experienced planter, you must realize that you do not have all the answers. This is my plantation, my home. And I will run it in the way I see best."

The older men looked shocked.

Lowell had a sneer on his face. "What did I tell you, Pa? This visit is a waste of time. He'll never listen to reason." His cup and saucer hit the table with a clatter. "We may as well be on our way."

"Please don't let me stop you." Jeremiah stood. "I wouldn't want to keep any of you from your busy lives."

"Well, I never." Mr. Fournier stood up and brushed his coat lapel free of crumbs with his handkerchief. "I suppose it's also true you're teaching your slaves to read and write?"

Jeremiah nodded.

"That is against the law, sir."

Jeremiah took a deep breath to steady himself. "As I said earlier, they are no longer slaves, and it is not against the law to educate free people."

The older man shook his head, his expression showing disgust. "You mark my words, LeGrand. You will not be allowed to continue flaunting our traditions. Don't make the mistake of ignoring our advice."

"I wouldn't dream of ignoring you, sir." Jeremiah opened the door and swept his hand in a wide arc. "But I will not be intimidated by someone just because he doesn't agree with my views." He called for the carriage and horses to be brought around and escorted his guests to the front porch. "Now if you will excuse me, gentlemen." He rolled up his sleeves and brushed past them, taking the front steps two at a time. "I have several jobs to finish before the day is over. Thank you for your visit."

Jeremiah knew his guests seethed as they departed, but he was determined to stand firm in what he truly felt God was leading him to do. No matter what any of them said or did.

twenty-seven

"And I'm not sure about inviting the Anderson family, my dear." Mrs. Sheffield's hazel eyes sharpened, reminding Alexandra of her betrothed.

Alexandra took her pen and carefully inscribed the name on the list. "I'm not sure I know them."

"That's not surprising. They do not have any children your age. Their oldest son, Charles, went to sea when he was just a lad. He doesn't come home often. And their girls, Catherine and Christine, married Kaintuck boatmen." She shook her head. "It was a terrible scandal because they chose husbands so far beneath them. I don't think their poor parents ever recovered."

Wondering if she'd been caught up in a nightmare, Alexandra pushed back an errant curl with one hand and held down the list of families with the other. She wanted to run away, but there was nowhere to go. So she sighed and turned her attention back to Lowell's mother. "I don't want to exclude anyone because of something in the past. I know only too well how hurtful that can be."

Mrs. Sheffield's eyes widened. "Oh, my dear, I'm sorry. I didn't think—" The older woman's cheeks reddened. "Of course we will invite them." She cleared her throat. "Is the wind getting too brisk? Perhaps we should move inside."

Alexandra accepted the change of subject in deference to Mrs. Sheffield's obvious dismay and glanced around. The gardens and the front lawn were beginning to come to life as spring chased away the freezing temperatures of winter. "I am enjoying the sunshine and the chirp of the birds."

Galloping hooves drowned out the sounds as Lowell and his father thundered down the lane toward the house and around to a side entrance without stopping. Mrs. Sheffield raised a hand in welcome, but neither man acknowledged her greeting.

Mrs. Sheffield looked at Alexandra, a forlorn smile on her face. "Mr. Sheffield and Lowell have been preoccupied of late."

"Should we go inside and find out what has happened?"

"Oh no, dear. You will find it's much better to leave the men alone at times like this. They would not appreciate our meddling. They will rush hither and yon making plans and devising strategies. And then the crisis will pass, and they will once again devote their time to us." She patted Alexandra's hand. "In the meantime, we have each other. Now, where were we?"

Alexandra looked down at the list, but her mind clanged a warning. Was this why Lowell did not seek or value her opinion in certain matters?

The front door opened, and she turned, a relieved smile on her face. Lowell must have decided to come out and greet her. But it was only the housekeeper wringing her hands on her apron. "Missus Sheffield, I need you inside, ma'am."

"What's wrong, Sally?" Mrs. Sheffield pushed back her chair. Alexandra started to rise, but she shook her head. "You stay out here. I'm sure I'll only be a minute or two."

Sitting back in her chair, Alexandra tried to recapture the peacefulness she had felt during her morning prayer, but it was impossible. She thought back to the days before her father had died. If she had not ignored his rushing hither and yon, things might have turned out differently. But with her awakened faith she knew she could not impose her own will on her father. God had lovingly given each person the right to choose whether to follow Him.

Yet she still could not rid herself of the notion that she might have been able to protect the victims of his crimes if she had just paid attention to the choices her father was making. She stood. She had no idea what was going on with the Sheffield men, but she would find out. She was determined not to make the same mistake again.

Raised voices drew her attention to one of the large windows. It must be coming from Mr. Sheffield's study. She was about to sweep past it when a name brought her up short.

"He is a menace to all of us." She recognized Lowell's voice. "Jeremiah LeGrand must be stopped. We tried it your way, Pa, but now you must see he will not listen to reason. He believes that freeing his slaves will not endanger the rest of us."

"There has to be a less violent way to convince him."

"It's either him or us." Someone pounded a fist on the wall next to the window where she was standing.

Alexandra jumped back, her heart hammering against her chest. After a moment, she forced herself back to the glass panes. She had to know what Lowell was proposing.

". . .late tonight, when all of them are asleep. If we burn down the house, he'll have no choice but to leave. It's his own fault. If he would only have agreed with us, we wouldn't be forced to take such extreme measures."

"Some people can't help being stubborn." Mr. Sheffield answered. "Just make sure you don't get caught."

"I won't, Pa."

Alexandra backed away from the window, a hand over her mouth. She wanted to march right into that study and tell both of the Sheffield men what she thought of their plans. But they would not listen. She could almost hear Lowell's condescending tones as he sent her back to his mother. No one else would listen to her, either, not until it was too late. It would be just like what happened to Papa. She had come full circle.

Frustration made her want to stomp her foot. What could she do? Threaten them with exposure? End her betrothal before disaster struck? Or was there something else she could do? Some way to stop them from succeeding? An idea popped into her mind, but Alexandra rejected it. It was too daring, too risky. But it might be the only way to avert disaster.

❧

The work he had accomplished today put him well ahead of his plans. Jeremiah was pleased. He was certain this season would be the best one ever at Magnolia Plantation, and with the steady increases in the price of cotton, all of his people should make a tidy profit. He put down the almanac he had been perusing, blew out the candle on his bedside table, and pulled the quilt up to his chin.

Sleep eluded him as he considered the next plan he wanted to implement. He could just imagine what the townspeople would say if they knew he planned to turn his plantation into an orphanage. But it was a dream God had given him, and now he had the perfect place to take care of children who would otherwise have nothing. He could almost hear their shouts and laughter as the orphans played and worked together. He would build a large classroom in the second floor of the main house, and he would hire a tutor or two to help with the instruction.

Excitement coursed through Jeremiah as he dreamed of his plans. He turned over and plumped his pillow before settling back down against it. Thanking God once again for the bounty, he closed his eyes and drifted to sleep.

The noise that woke him seemed to be an echo from his dreams. But then he heard it again—the whinny of a horse outside. The newly finished corral was too far from the house for him to hear those horses. He had a visitor. And most likely a visitor bent on mischief.

Jeremiah pushed the covers back and reached for his clothes. He dressed quickly and slipped out of the bedroom. He couldn't see much as he negotiated the staircase. Clouds had appeared in the sky as the sun set this evening, and now they played hide-and-seek with the moon. But he could hear the scrape of a window being raised. He followed the sound into the parlor at the same time as a shadowy figure stepped through and entered the room.

Instinct took over, and he launched himself at the miscreant, tackling him before he could use whatever weapon he held. His aim was true. His head contacted the intruder's torso at the waist and both of them went down in a tangle of skirts.

Skirts? Jeremiah's startled gaze fell on a delicate face ringed by dark curls. "Alexandra?" He rolled off her and bounded to his feet. "What is the meaning of this?"

She moaned and rolled into a ball.

Anger immediately turned into concern. "Are you hurt?"

"No." Her answer was muffled but emphatic.

"Have you become a burglar?" Another thought occurred to him. "Or are you so enamored of me that you cannot help yourself?"

Alexandra hissed and pulled herself into a sitting position. Cold moonlight illuminated her disdain. "Of course not. I came to warn you."

Jeremiah raised his eyebrows at her and crossed his arms over his chest. "Warn me? In the middle of the night? And of what? And sneaking around like some kind of thief. . . whatever the warning is, could you not have sent me a message?" He held out a hand to help her rise. "You're not carrying a weapon, are you?"

After a slight hesitation she put her hand in his. "Please try to refrain from idiotic questions. This is a serious matter."

Her glare made him grin. Now that she was on her feet, only a hairsbreadth separated them. Her perfume seemed to surround both of them. Suddenly his questions disappeared. All he could think of was how Alexandra reminded him of a ruffled kitten, soft and prickly and oh so appealing.

He wanted nothing more than to take her in his arms and kiss her until the glare in her eyes was replaced by a much more intimate look. What an inappropriate thought! It must be the enveloping darkness leading his mind down the wrong path.

Jeremiah backed away and looked toward the mantel for a

tinderbox. "Let's get a little light in here."

"No!" She put her hand on his arm. "If you do, they might see us."

"Who?" He looked out of the window she had just come through. "What are you talking about, Alexandra?"

"Lowell. He and some of the other planters are coming over here tonight to set your house on fire. I heard them talking this afternoon. They said it's the only way to control you."

It took him a moment to absorb the meaning of her words. "Are you sure?"

She nodded. "What are we going to do?"

Jeremiah caught her chin between his thumb and forefinger. She was so intent on helping him, but he could not allow her to put herself in danger. "*We* are not going to do anything. *You* are going to go back home, climb into your bed, and forget all about my problems. I will handle Lowell Sheffield."

When she opened her mouth to object, he swooped down and captured her lips with his own. He knew he shouldn't do it, knew he would regret it, but he couldn't resist the temptation. He would never again find himself alone with Alexandra.

For a brief instant, surprise held her still, but then she melted into him. It was the most miraculous thing he had ever experienced. The very air around them seemed to crackle with the emotions unleashed by their embrace.

It took him a moment to realize the crackling noise was coming from outside. He looked out of the window and saw gray smoke curling toward the house. Fear struck him like a bolt of lightning. "They must have set the hay barn on fire."

Jeremiah released her and ran out to the front porch. He could hear them now, whooping and hollering like a band of Indian warriors. He couldn't see the faces of the men as they rode off into the night, but he would worry about their identities later. For now, he had enough problems on his hands.

He prayed no one would get hurt as he rushed toward the well and released the bucket. It filled quickly, and he hoisted it upward. Pulling it from its hook, he ran toward the barn and tossed the water at the hungry flames. Then back to the well to start all over again.

Alexandra ran to the cast-iron bell on the far side of the house and jerked on its rope to set it ringing. The sound alerted the men and women who worked for him, and he soon found himself surrounded by eager hands. They formed a line from the well to the barn and passed bucket after bucket along. Jeremiah had no idea how long it took before the flames began to die back. He only knew that his hands were blistered and his shoulders ached.

As the sun began to rise in the eastern sky, the extent of the damage became obvious. He had lost the hay barn and the gin, and the weeds in one of the smaller fields had been scorched. He knew it could have been much worse. Would have been if not for the daring of a brave young woman.

He looked around until he spotted her helping some of the women and children search for hot cinders. Her dark hair cascaded around her shoulders, which drooped from exhaustion. Jeremiah thought she had never looked more beautiful.

He accepted a cup of cool water from a young girl and drank deeply. It tasted as sweet as honey to his parched lips. Taking a second cup from her, he strode to Alexandra. "It's time for you to stop." He thrust the cup toward her. "You've done more than enough."

She looked up at him, her face streaked with soot. "I'm so sorry, Jeremiah. I wish I'd gotten here sooner."

Jeremiah shook his head. "If not for you, I would have lost the whole place. And perhaps my life. You don't know how much I appreciate your willingness to put your reputation at risk by coming to warn me."

An odd look crossed her face. She took the cup and sipped from it. "God would not let me do any less."

Her words nearly brought him to his knees. He could not believe how badly he had misjudged this woman. The immature, spoiled debutante was an illusion. Alexandra Lewis was a woman of excellence. She epitomized all the qualities of the perfect helpmeet—intelligence, beauty, and faithfulness. Never mind her singed clothing and mussed hair, Jeremiah could not imagine any woman being more beautiful than Alexandra. Or more unattainable.

He clamped his jaws together. He'd better get her out of here right now before he decided he couldn't let her leave at all. Jeremiah turned away and waved to Oren. "See to it Miss Lewis gets home safely."

He walked away without a backward glance. She was not his to claim. She was betrothed to another.

twenty-eight

"Wake up." An unseen hand pulled back her quilt, and cool air swept over Alexandra. It was like being doused in cold water. Alexandra sat up and rubbed at her eyes.

"Mama?" She stared at the woman standing next to her bed, trying to sort through the fog of her tired mind. "What's wrong?"

"Your betrothed is downstairs demanding to see you right away."

"Lowell is here?" She pushed herself out of the bed, groaning when her aching feet hit the floor. She felt as though she'd been beaten. Every muscle in her body screamed abuse.

"Yes." Her mother pulled Alexandra's gown over her head and pushed her into a fresh petticoat. "Your grandmother sent me up here to help you get dressed, but we must hurry."

The clothes she had worn yesterday were piled in a corner of the room, a malodorous heap she would never again wear. Her mother tossed a questioning glance her way, but Alexandra had nothing to say. She didn't want to talk about what had happened last night. At least not until she'd had a chance to decide how to explain her actions.

With a sigh, her mother dragged a dress from her trunk, shaking it to release the wrinkles and hoisting it up over Alexandra's head.

As limp as a rag, Alexandra let her mother lace up the back of her dress and push her down onto the stool in front of her dressing table. "Ouch! Mama, slow down. What is so important?"

Her mother's mouth dropped open. "What's so important? Didn't you hear me? Lowell wants to see you right away."

Alexandra didn't protest further. Jemma came in and

dressed her hair. Alexandra was glad she had taken time to wash it out before climbing into bed last night. Even though it meant more tangles now, at least it no longer smelled of smoke. She endured the pulling and tugging of the brush as she considered what to say to Lowell. It was a good thing he was here so early. They could straighten out a few things right away.

"He's waiting for you in your grandfather's study." Mama led her downstairs and waved a hand in that direction. "Don't forget how much we're counting on him."

Alexandra pushed open the door, surprised to see Lowell ensconced behind her grandfather's desk. She let his effrontery slide, however. They had more important things to discuss.

"It's high time you got down here." Lowell's handsome face was a harsh mask. "Once we're married, I don't expect you to lie about in your bedchamber until mid-afternoon."

Alexandra marched to the front of the desk and stared down at him. "Is that so? Well, I have a thing—"

He interrupted her words. "Sit down. The reason I'm here is because I've received a report that you were seen coming home alone in another man's carriage, and I want an explanation."

Even if she had wanted to sit, Alexandra didn't think her rigid legs would allow it. She was appalled. "I'll stand, thank you. And as to my whereabouts, that should concern you since it's your fault I was not at home."

He stood up and came around to the front of the desk. "I'm listening." He took a stance directly in front of her, his hazel eyes as hard as marble.

Alexandra refused to back down in the face of his anger. She lifted her chin and squared her shoulders. "I was at Magnolia Plantation helping Jeremiah LeGrand put out the fire you and your cronies started."

Lowell's face paled as his expression changed from anger to shock. "Are you telling me you spent the night alone with an unmarried man?"

Jeremiah's embrace flashed through her mind. But she pushed it away. She had not gone to his house for that reason. "You are not listening to me, Lowell. I know you set that fire."

He snorted. "Of course I did, and I'm not ashamed to admit it to you, as I know you would not betray me. LeGrand needed to learn a lesson. The real question here is whether or not I should end our betrothal."

Alexandra drew herself up, ignoring the tender muscles in her back. "In that case, you have nothing to be concerned about. I won't marry you even if it means I have to scrub floors for the rest of my life."

Lowell's head snapped back as if she'd struck him. "You can't mean that. Not after my family supported you in spite of the scandal surrounding your father."

Alexandra raised her chin defiantly. "I apologize for any distress our association may have caused, but I promise you we will never be married. And if it were up to me, you would be facing the sheriff right now on a charge of arson." She sailed to the far side of the room, buoyed by the peace and strength surrounding her. "I'll be happy to call for your horse."

"I can't believe it." Lowell's voice reflected his shock as he stumbled across the room.

Alexandra almost felt sorry for him. He probably had never dreamed anyone would flout his family's money and influence.

At one time, he would have been right, but that time was behind her. Now she followed a Higher Power. She would rest in the knowledge God loved her and had a wonderful plan for her future.

twenty-nine

Jeremiah knocked on the Sheffields' front door and waited for it to swing open. The tall, thin, black man who opened the door accepted his card and left Jeremiah in the hallway. A clock ticked the minutes away while he waited.

Finally the black man returned. "Right this way, Master LeGrand."

Jeremiah followed him to a large library where both Sheffield and his son sat. After the greetings, he was invited to take a seat.

"Have you reconsidered your position, Mr. LeGrand?" Lowell sprawled across a horsehair sofa.

"Not at all." Jeremiah's eyes narrowed, and he reached for the man's right hand. "Is that a burn?"

Lowell jerked his hand away. "I burned myself putting a log on the fire this morning."

Jeremiah nodded and turned to his father. "I'm sure you understand that I can ruin your family if I go to the sheriff. While I may not have seen exactly who was at my house last night, after I report the conversation we had, he will be looking at you and your son very closely for evidence of wrongdoing."

Father and son exchanged a glance. "What do you want?" Mr. Sheffield was the one to ask the question.

"I want a formal, written confession from your son. Rest assured that it will never see the light of day as long as nothing like this ever happens again."

Mr. Sheffield opened a drawer in front of him and pulled out a piece of stationery that he shoved toward his son.

"Pa! You know the sheriff won't listen to the likes of him."

"That may be true, Lowell, but I told you not to get caught. You're too hotheaded, too certain your good looks and connections will get you free of any problems. That little Lewis gal knows it, too. That's probably why she broke off your engagement. You should be glad Mr. LeGrand is giving you this chance. I would hate for a son of mine to risk being branded a criminal."

Jeremiah kept his gaze fixed on an intricate silver candelabrum, but his mind was whirling. Alexandra had ended her betrothal? Was it because of last night? Because of their embrace? His heart thudded in his chest. Suddenly the confession young Sheffield was penning seemed insignificant.

Mr. Sheffield continued to harangue his son, recounting every failure and setback in Lowell's life. By the time Lowell was done writing, Jeremiah almost felt sorry for him. But then he looked at the blisters on his own hands. He had to protect himself and those who depended on him.

Lowell signed the sheet with a flourish and handed it to Jeremiah, who glanced at it briefly before folding the document and placing it in his coat pocket. "Thank you, gentlemen." He stood up. "I'll find my own way out."

He flung himself onto the back of his horse and galloped away from the Sheffields' home as though enemy soldiers were chasing him. All he could think of was seeing Alexandra. He had to find out why she had ended her engagement. He had to know if he had a chance.

੦

Alexandra sat on the piano bench and stared blindly at the sheet music perched in front of her. She had told her family her marriage plans had been cancelled, but she had not offered any reason.

Grand-mère had blasted her with threats, but when Alexandra refused to be cowered, she had finally given up and retired to her bedroom. Aunt Patricia and Uncle John had congratulated her on standing her ground and told her they would help if she needed it. Mama had cried a little, but then she had hugged Alexandra and confessed that Lowell was a bit overbearing. Cousin Percival harrumphed twice and toddled off.

Now she sought time alone to gather her thoughts and seek God's guidance.

"Your hands must not be as sore as mine if you can play a song." The deep drawl made her gasp.

The piano bench squeaked as she pivoted.

There he stood, tall as a cedar and immovable as stone. A lock of his thick hair had drifted across his forehead, and her fingers longed to comb it back. His blue eyes burned with the heat of summer, igniting an answering fire in her soul.

"Jeremiah—I mean, Mr. LeGrand. It's good to see you."

He turned from her, and Alexandra's heart plummeted. Did he despise her so? She had been very forward in going to his home. But what else could she have done? "Did you lose much in the fire?"

He twisted back to face her, and Alexandra's gaze searched his expression for a clue to his feelings.

"No, thank God. Nothing that cannot be replaced." His voice was rough. He cleared his throat. "I went to see Lowell and his father."

Alexandra tipped her head to one side. "Why would you do that?"

"I wanted to make certain my home would be safe in the future." A smile made the dimples in his cheeks appear. "I didn't want you having to rush to my rescue again."

"I didn't do much." Alexandra hid her blistered hands behind her skirt. "No more than anyone else would have done."

He stepped toward her, a strange light in his eyes. "I don't know anyone who would have been as brave as you were."

The air seemed to leave the room in a rush. Alexandra put a hand to her chest. "You give me too much credit."

"Alexandra, this is not what I came to talk about."

She took a shallow breath. "It's not?"

He shook his head and more hair fell across his forehead. "I. . ." His voice faltered.

Alexandra watched his throat work, wishing she could think of something to say to ease his discomfort. Was he going to apologize for embracing her? Or was some other matter troubling him?

"You may have heard about the changes at Magnolia Plantation."

She nodded and watched him pace across the room before returning to stand in front of her.

"I have so many ideas I still want to implement, but I've realized lately I need help in doing that. A helpmeet who shares my enthusiasm for reaching out to others." He stopped and looked up at the ceiling. "Besides offering opportunities to the people working at the plantation, I've always dreamed of creating a haven for orphaned children who have no one else to care for them." His gaze returned to her face. "How would you feel about being a part of those changes?"

A gasp of pleasure filled Alexandra. "I'd love to be a part of—" The squeakiness in her voice surprised her. Suddenly her throat didn't want to work. She swallowed hard and started again. "I've changed greatly over the past months. I've learned about the importance of giving to others, caring for those who are not as blessed as I."

His dimples peeked out as his lips curved upward. "I've seen firsthand how much you've changed. You are the one I want to share my life with. Please tell me it's not too late. Tell me you don't love Lowell Sheffield."

She flew off the bench and into his arms, burrowing into his shoulder with a sob. Jeremiah's arms wrapped around her, drawing her close and making her feel safe. All of her concerns and doubts melted away. "I don't love him, Jeremiah. How could I when you hold my heart in your hands?"

"Are you sure you can be happy with a simple farmer?"

"Only if his name is Jeremiah LeGrand." She lifted her face then and let him see the love she felt. How had she ever entertained marriage to anyone else? As their lips met, she sent a prayer of thanksgiving to God. What a joyous thing to follow His bidding.

epilogue

Magnolia Plantation, December 1817

"Be careful, Charlotte." Alexandra admonished Judah and Susannah's toddler as she lurched toward the tall Christmas tree. "We don't want you to scratch that beautiful face of yours." Alexandra caught up with the little girl before she could reach the other children and led her in the opposite direction, across the ballroom floor to where Susannah sat.

"Thank you." Susannah pushed herself up from the sofa with one hand, the other cradling her slumbering newborn. "I don't know how Charlotte gets away from me so easily."

Judah and Jeremiah emerged from the far side of the tree, where they had been engaged in keeping the large fir steady while it was being decorated by orphaned boys and girls from ages three to six. Alexandra and Jeremiah had taken them in when an epidemic of yellow fever swept through Natchez and were taking care of them until permanent homes for them could be found.

"It's not as if you don't have your hands full." Judah smiled at his wife and took the infant from her, cradling the little girl in the crook of his arm. Alexandra was glad he no longer needed his crutches. The wooden leg he used allowed him so much more freedom to move about.

Her attention was caught when three-year-old Katie, the youngest of the orphan children, plopped down in the middle of the floor and began to cry.

"Whatever is the matter, Katie?" She glanced at the other five children, who were still running back and forth with strands of berries and homemade decorations for the tree. "Did someone push her down?"

Deborah Trent, the oldest of the children, stepped forward. A very serious little girl, she mothered the rest of the youngsters, none of whom were related to her. She put her arms around Katie and whispered in her ear until the little girl stopped crying.

Alexandra was thankful Deborah was so good with the children. It seemed she had so little energy herself these days.

The year had been hard for Natchez, but they still had a lot to celebrate. On December 10, Mississippi had become the twentieth state to enter the union, the new government meeting in the nearby town of Washington until the epidemic left Natchez, now the state capital. Their neighbors were beginning to tolerate her husband's progressive ideas about sharecropping, if not adopting the practice itself. And they had been able to make Jeremiah's dream of providing for orphaned children come true. She smiled across the room at him and thanked God once again for uniting them. She could hardly wait to see his face when she gave him his gift this year.

He walked over to her and dropped a kiss on her forehead. "I love you, dearest."

"I love you, too, my darling husband." The look in his eyes still had the power to make her heart flutter. She was the most blessed woman in the world. Thankfulness filled her. She had come so close to allowing her grandmother to bully her into the wrong marriage. Only by following God's will had she managed to find the true path to happiness. "Will you read the Christmas story to us now? Or after we exchange gifts?"

He pointed his chin at the large Bible that rested in a place of honor on top of her writing table. "Let's remind our children of the real reason for this celebration."

They gathered everyone around, the children, their friends, and all of the people who worked for and with them. The large ballroom was quite crowded, but there was no noise as everyone listened to her husband read from the second chapter of Luke.

After the reading was finished, everyone received a gift, from the youngest sharecropper's child to Ezekiel, the oldest member of the household. Alexandra received a pair of gloves and a shawl from the Hugheses, as well as several hand-drawn pictures from the children.

When the rest of the gifts were distributed, Jeremiah moved toward her, his hands behind his back. "I have a special gift for you, my love."

He brought his hands around, and she saw what appeared to be a scroll tied with a black ribbon. "What is it?" She took the roll from him and loosened the string. Smoothing the papers in her lap, she glanced at the opening paragraphs. "Is this a deed?"

"Yes." His smile widened, making his dimples appear. "Do you remember the house in town that we looked at a few weeks back?"

Excitement coursed through her. "You bought it?" The papers slid to the floor when she jumped up and threw her arms around his neck, thinking of the Georgian mansion with expansive grounds that could be converted into a homey and comfortable orphanage to house a dozen unfortunate children. "You are undoubtedly the most splendid husband in the world."

"How can I not be when I have such a wonderful wife?" He held her in a tight hug. "I still cannot believe how much God has blessed us, Alexandra. Beyond my fondest dreams."

"Mine, too, my dearest." She smiled up at him. "I have a gift for you."

He let her go long enough to reach for the small package on the side table next to the sofa where she had been sitting. "That looks too small to be for me."

The others in the room seemed to fade away as Alexandra watched him unwrap the paper to uncover a tiny knitted cap. "It is too small for you."

Recognition like the first rays of dawn filled his face. "A baby?"

A blush filled her face as she nodded. "Yes."

"Should you be standing up?" Concern replaced the wonder in his expression. "Shouldn't you be resting? Here, sit down."

Judah's laughter drew a frown from Jeremiah. "She's not quite that delicate yet."

"Leave him alone." Susannah elbowed her husband. "I still remember when you were that attentive to me."

Judah stroked his chin. "That was just yesterday, wasn't it?"

They all laughed.

Alexandra felt as light as a puff of air. She never would have dreamed her life could be so filled with joy and laughter, hope and happiness. As her husband raised her hand to his lips, she knew that no matter what the future held God would see her and her faith-filled husband through it all.

A Letter To Our Readers

Dear Reader:

In order that we might better contribute to your reading enjoyment, we would appreciate your taking a few minutes to respond to the following questions. We welcome your comments and read each form and letter we receive. When completed, please return to the following:

Fiction Editor
Heartsong Presents
PO Box 719
Uhrichsville, Ohio 44683

1. Did you enjoy reading *Across the Cotton Fields* by Diane Ashley and Aaron McCarver?
   ❑ Very much! I would like to see more books by this author!
   ❑ Moderately. I would have enjoyed it more if

   _____

   _____

   _____

2. Are you a member of **Heartsong Presents**? ❑ Yes ❑ No
   If no, where did you purchase this book? _____

   _____

3. How would you rate, on a scale from 1 (poor) to 5 (superior), the cover design? _____

4. On a scale from 1 (poor) to 10 (superior), please rate the following elements.

   ____ Heroine   ____ Plot
   ____ Hero   ____ Inspirational theme
   ____ Setting   ____ Secondary characters

5. These characters were special because? _____
   _____
   _____

6. How has this book inspired your life? _____
   _____
   _____

7. What settings would you like to see covered in future
   Heartsong Presents books? _____
   _____
   _____

8. What are some inspirational themes you would like to see
   treated in future books? _____
   _____
   _____

9. Would you be interested in reading other **Heartsong
   Presents** titles? ❑ Yes ❑ No

10. Please check your age range:
    ❑ Under 18   ❑ 18-24
    ❑ 25-34   ❑ 35-45
    ❑ 46-55   ❑ Over 55

Name _____
Occupation _____
Address _____
City, State, Zip_____
E-mail _____

Doctor *in* Petticoats

Training as a nurse, Beth dreams of serving the people of her town suffering without a doctor. When she meets a doctor deserting from the army, she finds they work well together. But can she give up her dreams of doctoring and help rid his demons so that he can heal again?

Historical, paperback, 320 pages, 5⅞" x 8"

Please send me ____ copies of *Doctor in Petticoats*. I am enclosing $12.99 for each. (Please add $4.00 to cover postage and handling per order. OH add 7% tax. If outside the U.S. please call 740-922-7280 for shipping charges.)

Name _____

Address _____

City, State, Zip _____

Heart❤ong

Any 12
Heartsong
Presents titles
for only
$27.00*

HISTORICAL ROMANCE IS CHEAPER BY THE DOZEN!

Buy any assortment of twelve *Heartsong Presents* titles and save 25% off of the already discounted price of $2.97 each!

*plus $4.00 shipping and handling per order and sales tax where applicable. If outside the U.S. please call 740-922-7280 for shipping charges.

HEARTSONG PRESENTS TITLES AVAILABLE NOW:

(If ordering from this page, please remember to include it with the order form.)

Presents

Great Inspirational Romance at a Great Price!

Heartsong Presents books are inspirational romances in contemporary and historical settings, designed to give you an enjoyable, spirit-lifting reading experience. You can choose wonderfully written titles from some of today's best authors like Wanda E. Brunstetter, Mary Connealy, Susan Page Davis, Cathy Marie Hake, Joyce Livingston, and many others.

When ordering quantities less than twelve, above titles are $2.97 each.
Not all titles may be available at time of order.